P9-DIE-839

Finding Jack

Finding Jack

GARETH CROCKER

ST. MARTIN'S PRESS
New York

This is a work of fiction. All of the characters, organizations, and events portrayed in this novel are either products of the author's imagination or are used fictitiously.

 Printed in the United States of America. For information, address St. Martin's Press, 175 Fifth Avenue, New York, N.Y. 10010.

www.stmartins.com

www.garethcrocker.com

Design by Kathryn Parise

LIBRARY OF CONGRESS CATALOGING-IN-PUBLICATION DATA

Crocker, Gareth.
(Leaving Jack)
Finding Jack : a novel / Gareth Crocker. — 1st ed.
p. cm.
Originally published as Leaving Jack. Johannesburg, South Africa : Robert Hale Publishers, 2008.
ISBN 978-0-312-62172-8
1. Soldiers—Fiction. 2. Dogs—War use—Fiction. 3. Human-animal relationships—Fiction. 4. Bereavement—Fiction. 5. Vietnam War, 1961–1975—Fiction. I. Title.
PR9369.4.C76L43 2011
823'.92—dc22 2010039361

First Edition: February 2011

10 9 8 7 6 5 4 3 2 1

For beautiful Kerry. MAYVTW.

And for the dogs that never made it home.

Acknowledgments

Special and heartfelt thanks to my U.S. agent, James Schiavone of the Schiavone Literary Agency, and to my editor at St. Martin's Press, the simply divine Nichole Argyres.

Thank you both for taking a chance on me.

And for believing in Jack.

Finding Jack

Prologue

Chicago
12 January 1972

The wind sulked around Hampton Lane cemetery like a child lamenting the loss of a favorite toy. It stirred the crisp autumn leaves lining the many cobbled paths, but did little more than tow them along slowly, like condemned souls being dragged to the afterlife.

Standing among the rolling fields of dead in a sea of granite and marble tombstones, Fletcher Carson trudged toward the foot of a tree where his life lay buried under two stark stone crosses. His wife, Abigail, had been such a positive person that she had seldom discussed death, a reluctance underlined by the loss of her parents barely a year ago. Only during the drawing up of their wills did it emerge that she wished to be interred under the shade of a maple tree with only a simple cross to mark her final resting place. Her epitaph was every word as humble as she was. It read:

HERE RESTS ABIGAIL CARSON, LOVING WIFE AND MOTHER.
MAY HER LIGHT NEVER FADE FROM OUR HEARTS.

Kelly's cross was half the size of her mother's. It carried only her name and the dates of her short life. When it came down to it, and despite being a writer for most of his working life, Fletcher hadn't been able to commission a message. The right words, he was certain, did not exist.

"Fletcher." A voice drifted toward him. "I thought I'd find you here."

Fletcher immediately recognized the broad Southern drawl. It was Marvin Samuels, his editor and possibly only remaining friend in the world.

"You look good," Marvin remarked, but the inflection in his voice suggested otherwise. At just under six feet, Fletcher Carson was by no means a particularly tall man, but there was a stoop in his posture now that belied his true height. He was blessed with smooth olive skin, thick black hair, and hazel eyes like large nuggets of carved oak. A distinctive cleftlike scar in the middle of his chin did little to detract from his good looks. At twenty-nine, he was in the prime of his life, but the burden of the recent months weighed heavily on him. His athletic build remained, but his face carried the expression of a man who had wandered into a dark labyrinth and long since abandoned hope of ever finding his way out.

"I read somewhere that the dead can hear you," Fletcher said, staring at the ground.

"I'm sorry?"

"They say that if someone they really loved visits their grave, they can hear that person's thoughts. It can be raining or blowing a gale around the cemetery, but just around their grave, everything becomes still. That's when they're listening."

"I hope it's true."

Fletcher slipped his hands into his pockets. "Why have you come here, Marvin?"

"Why do you ask questions you know the answers to?"

"We've been through this; there's nothing left to discuss. I'm leaving tomorrow."

"You know your mother's going out of her mind with worry? I can't keep making excuses for you. When are you going to return her calls?"

"We keep missing each other."

"Like hell you do."

"It's complicated, Marvin. Please stay out of it."

Marvin folded his arms and looked up at the sky. "Sure. I'll just stand around and watch while you try to get yourself killed."

"I'm asking you to respect my decision."

"Do you think this is what your girls would've wanted?"

Fletcher snapped his head around, anger curling up a corner of his mouth. "You're in no position to ask that. Do you have any idea what the last few months have been like?"

"Of course not, but going off to fight in Vietnam isn't the answer."

"What if it were Cathy or Cynthia? What would you do?"

"I'd try to find a way to get over their passing and carry on with my life."

"Really?" Fletcher said, swallowing hard, and then pointing to his daughter's grave. "Kelly was barely seven, Marvin. How do you get over that? If you know, please enlighten me."

"Fletcher—"

"Tell me something," he went on, his voice faltering, "do you know where the line is?"

"The line?"

"Where you end . . . and your family begins."

"C'mon, don't do this."

"I'll tell you. There is no line. I understand that now. You're one entity, and when a part of you is cut away, the rest of you slowly bleeds out."

"Jesus, Fletcher."

"Our soldiers are being massacred in Vietnam. Most of them are still kids. They've got their whole lives ahead of them. It makes sense that people like me enlist."

"People like you," Marvin repeated. "You mean people who want to die. You need help, Fletcher, you need to speak to a professional."

"A shrink? Will that bring back my girls?"

"It might help you to learn to cope without them."

"That's just it," Fletcher said, shaking his head. "I don't want to cope without them."

Marvin tried to reply, but could draw on nothing meaningful to say.

"I appreciate you coming and all that you've done for me, but I think you should leave."

"Just let me—"

"Please," Fletcher whispered. "Just go."

Marvin began to walk away, then stopped. "Do you remember that piece you did on suicide when you were still covering hospitals? At the end, you wrote that if only the sufferers had been able to see past the moment of their pain, they could claw their way back to life."

"What I didn't realize at the time," Fletcher replied, his voice thin, "is that you can never truly understand things that haven't happened to you."

Marvin stared up at the sky. "I've stood by you through this whole goddamn nightmare. From the moment the plane went down to the day you were discharged from the hospital. If you leave tomorrow, then I've just been wasting my time."

"I'm sorry, Marvin, but this isn't about you. I've made my decision."

"Fine, but know that this is the last thing your girls would've wanted for you. You're making a terrible mistake."

"Maybe . . . but it's mine to make."

Marvin turned away, shaking his head. "You're heading into a nightmare. It's hell over there."

Fletcher nodded slowly and pictured his girls beneath his feet. "It's hell everywhere," he whispered.

When Marvin was gone, Fletcher knelt down between the two graves. He reached into his pocket and pulled out a silver frame Abigail had kept on her bedside table. It held one of her favorite photos of the three of them, sitting on a large boulder in Yellowstone Park. He gently placed it down on the plot of fresh grass covering her grave. From another pocket, he withdrew a small wooden box, which he rested against the foot of Kelly's cross. In it was a crystal sculpture of the dog he had promised to buy her. She had died three days before her seventh birthday.

It was the present she would never have.

PART I

The Land of Ghosts

One

Death Valley, Vietnam
Six months later
6 July 1972

Only the top half of Fletcher's head was visible above the murky water. The rest of his body was submerged beneath the mud and thick reeds alongside the riverbank. He was drawing short, shallow breaths. From his position, he could make out three members of his platoon. Point man Mitchell Lord, radioman Gunther Pearson, and their lieutenant, Rogan Brock, were hidden in a classic L-shaped ambush awaiting an enemy patrol. They had been hiking up to a site three kilometers away to set up a landing zone when they were warned about them. Their information had the group at a little more than twenty soldiers—large by Vietnam standards. The fact that their own platoon numbered only half that was of no real consequence, as the ambush, coupled with their superior firepower, gave them a telling advantage. Their chief concern was that many Vietnamese patrols comprised small groups of soldiers staggered sometimes half a kilometer apart. There was a real danger that during the firefight, they would be outflanked.

Fletcher blinked away the sweat around his eyes and checked his rifle again. There was always a chance, however vague, that it would jam and leave him defenseless at the vital moment. As sniper, his job was to try to pick out the ranking officer and take him down first. Cut off the head, and the body will fall, the army taught them. It was the same modus operandi for both sides, and as such, none of the soldiers wore any insignia out in the field that would reveal their rank. But there were other ways of telling. Often the soldier consulting the map would be the ranking officer. Regardless, it was crucial that Fletcher allowed the point man to pass in front of him. If Fletcher fired too soon, the soldiers would have a chance to scatter and find cover. Another problem was that both the North Vietnamese Army and the Vietcong, or Charlie, as U.S. soldiers nicknamed them, were extremely smart and notoriously elusive. On one of Fletcher's first tours, several weeks before, they had set up an identical ambush on a patrol of sixteen Charlie, yet several of them had escaped. Given their position and superior firepower, the trap had seemed watertight, but there was a leak somewhere. An unseen hole through which some of the soldiers had managed to disappear. By the time the last of the rounds had been fired and the rifle smoke began to lift, only twelve men were left dead on the ground. In fact, so slippery was Charlie that some U.S. troops had been on tour for months and had never even seen him, although most had felt him. He was small, nimble, and blended seamlessly into the jungle. His tactics were to attack and retreat—basic guerrilla warfare. No helicopters, gunships, or bombing campaigns to support him. Just cunning and cutting. He would stab you and then withdraw into the shadows. Charlie was a ghost that never slept. He made traps that intended to maim, not kill. Traps that would slow down platoons and gnaw away at their spirit. In the jungles of Vietnam, Charlie was a highly formidable enemy.

Faint voices.

Fletcher narrowed his gaze to hide the whites of his eyes. He remained perfectly still, the area around him disturbed only by a swarm of flying insects breaking the surface of the soupy water with their wings in an attempt to lure out prey.

It seems everyone's hunting, he thought grimly. The body of his gun was covered with mud and rotting leaves to guard against reflections. Only the open barrel—the killing eye, as they called it—was visible to the trail.

Footsteps and voices. Louder now.

A soldier, barely five feet tall and wearing a worn pith helmet, emerged over the rise. Holding his breath, Fletcher curled his finger around the trigger of his M16 and followed the diminutive figure as he approached the ambush. Something slick and heavy swam between his legs. Still no sign of the rest of the patrol.

Waiting . . . waiting.

Fletcher flinched at what he saw next. An American soldier wearing the distinctive emblem of the First Air Cavalry Division appeared into view. His arms were bound over a wooden pole behind his back, and his face bore the obvious signs of interrogation. As he limped forward slowly, he was kicked from behind by one of his captors.

Fletcher looked to his lieutenant for instruction. Through a series of hand signals, Rogan ordered him to take out the two soldiers directly in front of and behind the hostage. This would minimize the chance of the American getting shot in the firefight. He then signaled for the rest of the platoon to switch from automatic to single fire. He looked back at Fletcher and held up his fist, waiting for the right moment.

A bead of sweat rolled down the bridge of Fletcher's nose, paused for a beat, then dropped into the water. With one eye on Rogan and the other straining toward his two marks, he again held his breath. *C'mon . . . c'mon . . .*

Rogan dropped his hand.

Fletcher squeezed off two rounds in quick succession. Before the second soldier even hit the ground, the rest of the platoon opened fire. The sound was devastating. As Charlie tried to return fire, point man Mitchell Lord burst out of his hiding place, tackled the U.S. hostage, and dragged him down an embankment. It was typical Lord. He was every bit as brave as he was crazy. Toward the back of the patrol, three of the soldiers had managed to find cover, but they were quickly flanked and taken out. In less than a minute, twenty-three Charlie lay dead in the burning sunshine of Vietnam.

Just another day in hell.

Two

After a quick sweep of the area to ensure that there were no splinter patrols nearby, Fletcher's closest friend in the platoon, infantryman Travis Tucker, untied the hostage. He appeared badly dehydrated; his tongue was so swollen, he could barely speak. Only after several generous sips of water was he able to relay some basic information. He was a helicopter pilot who had been shot down while dropping a platoon into a hot zone. He was the sole survivor. He had been held hostage for more than a week and taken to three different camps, where he'd been interrogated and tortured each time. Sometimes they would ask their questions in Vietnamese, knowing full well he couldn't answer. In Vietnam, the most horrific things passed for humor. His hands were shaking so badly, he could barely hold the water canister up to his mouth. Each sip seemed to improve his pallor though, as if the canister wasn't filled with water, but rather a skin-toned ink that was being infused into his body.

"Easy with that," Rogan warned. "He'll bring it all up." From a physical perspective, few men registered a more imposing presence than Rogan Brock. Although tall and heavily built, he was not the largest man in Vietnam, but there was something deeply unsettling behind his stare. There was a sense of raw aggression lurking beyond the black centers of his eyes. His shaven head and pitted face added additional threat to his appearance.

The pilot wiped his mouth with the side of his torn sleeve. "I can't tell you how grateful I am. Jesus . . . *thank you*. I'm pretty sure they were going to kill me today. From what I could make out, we had one more stop to make. One more interrogation, and they were going to put a bullet in my face. How'd you know where to find me?"

The question saddened Fletcher. In his delirious state, the pilot believed that what had just transpired was a planned rescue. The truth was that the U.S. was having enough of a battle just trying to keep a foothold in the war without having to coordinate rescue attempts for POWs.

"Forget about it. The important thing is that you're safe now. We'll have you back at base tomorrow morning, where you can get some rest. The name's Travis, by the way. Travis Tucker."

"Will Peterson," he replied, accepting Travis's hand.

"Let me introduce you to the rest of the Fat Lady."

"The Fat Lady? I've heard of you guys. You were part of the company that survived that shitstorm outside Kon Tum. The story I heard had you outnumbered eight to one."

"More like four to one, and we didn't all survive. We lost three men that day," Rogan fired back. "You shouldn't believe everything you hear."

Travis moved quickly to defuse the moment. "This, as you might've already guessed, is our lieutenant, the charismatic Rogan Brock. The man sitting next to you is probably the third best sniper within a hundred yards from here, Fletcher Carson."

"Definitely top ten." Fletcher nodded.

"Radioman Gunther Pearson . . . squad leader Wayville Rex . . . weapons specialist Kingston Lane . . . infantryman Arnold Keens . . . medic Edgar Green . . . and infantryman Craig Fallow."

More handshakes and nods.

"And this," Travis continued, "is the madman who dragged you down the embankment. The finest point man in all of Vietnam: Mitchell Lord."

Mitchell stepped right up to Will's face so that their noses almost touched. His eyes were open wide, unnaturally so. "Please call me Mitch. Only the ladies call me Lord . . . or Jesus Christ, if the feeling grabs them," he said, winking one eye then the other.

"Well, thank you . . . Mitch, that was some brave shit you pulled there."

Mitchell frowned, as if he didn't understand the comment, and turned away.

"All right, ladies, now that we've exchanged phone numbers, we need to get moving," Rogan cut in. "There's still a fucking war going on here."

They picked up their gear while Fletcher and Travis helped Will to his feet. As they moved out, Kingston Lane began to hum a tune. A few of the men joined in.

"What's this?"

"Every time we make it through a firefight, Kingston hums this hymn," Fletcher replied.

"Like some sort of victory song?"

"It's really just to give thanks that we didn't lose anyone and to let off some steam."

"It sounds familiar."

"It's an old Christian hymn called 'By His Hand.'"

"I like it."

Fletcher smiled, but chose not to reply. Instead, he allowed the tune into his heart. It couldn't cure their ills, he knew, but it sometimes helped dull the pain.

"Tell me," Will asked as the hymn ended, "why do you call yourselves the Fat Lady?"

"Wayville, why do we call ourselves the Fat Lady?" Fletcher called out.

"Because Vietnam ain't over, baby . . . till the Fat Lady sings! Hoohah!"

They all laughed until Rogan spun around. "We having fun, platoon? Should we light a few flares to make the VC's job a little easier? Carson, I don't want to hear another goddamn word from you until we hit the LZ. Do you understand me?"

Fletcher tipped the brim of his helmet, sarcastically so.

Rogan had a habit of singling him out for abuse whenever he was unhappy with the platoon. The reason, Fletcher suspected, was because a mild dilution of Asian blood flowed through his veins and because he bore some, albeit fleeting, resemblance to the Vietcong. In the outside world, his good looks opened doors for him. But this was Vietnam, and given the side he was fighting on, occasionally his olive skin and coal black hair incensed his countrymen.

After a while, Fletcher whispered ahead to Gunther Pearson, who was radioing through news of the ambush and subsequent rescue. "How much farther to the landing zone?"

"Around two clicks."

"How far?" Will asked quietly.

"Two kilometers. Do you think you can make it?" Travis asked.

"Make it? I'll fucking race you there."

Three

Using entrenching tools, the platoon had soon dug several foxholes and rigged the surrounding area with trip wires linked to mines and flares. Fortunately they were in a clearing on top of a small hillock and didn't need to remove any trees. Most of the soldiers constructed hooches above their foxholes—makeshift tents created by zipping two ponchos together. Once all the work was done and their coordinates radioed in to base for the morning pickup, Rogan called the platoon together for a short debriefing. Afterwards, he turned his attention to guard duty. "Fallow and Green, you're on watch until 2200. Carson and Tucker till 0300. Rex and Lane, you relieve them till sunrise."

Travis raised his hands to his head. "C'mon, that's two nights in a row."

"On second thought, Rex and Lane, you're only to relieve Mrs. Tucker and Mrs. Carson at 0330." He waited for a response and, when there was none forthcoming, rubbed salt into the wound. "You should be more selective of the company you keep, Tucker. The people you side with can really bring you down."

"Then may I share a foxhole with you, lieutenant?" Travis asked.

Rogan had already turned and was walking away.

"Please, sir, can't I sleep with you tonight? I'll give you a back rub. A foot massage. We can even share my sleeping bag! Let's see where it takes us."

Rogan raised his middle finger and kept walking.

"Shit," Travis sighed. "I'd like to shoot him in the ass."

Fletcher shook his head. "Fucking graveyard again."

Mitchell Lord stood up and ran his fingers through his long black hair. How he was allowed to keep it that length was something of a mystery. "I'll take over for you guys."

"Thanks, Mitch, but if Rogan finds out you're covering for us, he'll piss himself," Fletcher said.

Mitchell was hardly ever assigned to guard duty, not because Rogan necessarily favored him, but because they couldn't afford to have him tired in his position as point man. Running point required an inordinate amount of skill and concentration. It entailed going ahead of the patrol, checking for traps, ambushes, enemy patrols, animal tracks, and even searching for secure pathways. It was also physically taxing, as he had to navigate and hack his way through long stretches of dense jungle with a machete. To have him up on watch was not only unfair, but also risky for the platoon. One of the reasons they had suffered relatively so few casualties was because of Mitchell's ability to sniff out danger.

At their foxhole, Travis removed his boots and sat down next to Fletcher, settling into as comfortable a position as he could find. He pushed his glasses onto the top of his head, which apart from a light sprinkling of wispy brown hair, was largely bald. Although not a particularly handsome man, he was blessed with piercingly blue eyes and a kind and open face that people responded to. For a while they spoke about Will Peterson and the firefight, but gradually their conversation meandered away from the day's events.

"Fletcher, there's something I've been wanting to ask you for a while now. I know I've got no right to ask it, and I'll understand if you tell me to shut up and mind my own business, but . . . I—"

"You want to know about the crash?'

Travis nodded hesitantly, with the care of a man prodding a sleeping lion with a stick.

Fletcher propped up his rifle against the side of the hole and stared out over the jungle. "The *Odyssey* was billed as a revolution in air travel. Do you know that it took ten years to design and was capable of holding almost six hundred passengers?"

"I remember," Travis replied softly. "It was all over the press."

"You should've seen her, Trav. She was as big as a ship. Almost three hundred and fifty feet nose to tail, with a wingspan as wide as a football field. She had six engines and weighed just over five hundred and fifty tons. She was designed to fly supersonic at a range of ten thousand miles. Although," he said, trailing off, "they never did prove that . . ."

"What brought her down?"

"A design flaw in the fuel system was the last I heard, but it doesn't matter. All that counts is that she came down. There were three hundred and twenty-seven passengers on board its maiden flight, and only nine of us survived."

Fletcher paused, steeling himself. When he spoke again, his voice seemed to flatten out and his eyes fixed on a faraway place, well beyond the jungle. "As one of the journalists invited to the launch, I was allowed to bring my family along for the ride. We had just reached our cruising altitude when the pilot invited all the children to the flight deck. Kelly was about to step into the cockpit when the door was slammed in her face and the children were all rushed back to their seats. The cabin crew told us to put on our safety belts and refused to say anything more. About a minute later, an engine on the right wing seemed to stutter—it felt like a cough—and then exploded. Another two on the left wing followed moments later. I remember trying to hold on to Abby and Kelly as the plane fell . . . telling them that everything was going to be okay . . . that the plane had backup systems, but I knew we were in serious trouble. And then . . . and then there was nothing. I woke up still strapped to my seat, lying in someone's backyard. I remember the grass was freshly mowed; I can still smell it. A section of the plane's wing and one of its engines had landed no more than fifty yards away from me. The burning jet fuel had lit up a large oak tree in the corner of the property. Beyond it, through a collapsed section of wall, I could see what was left of the plane's fuselage. It was lying in an open field about a mile away. The flames were as high as church steeples . . . I knew then that my girls were gone."

"Jesus," Travis whispered, taking a minute to process the story. "And that's why you decided to enlist?"

"Not right away. The day after the funeral, I decided to kill myself," he offered matter-of-factly. "I threw myself off the sixth floor of the hospital where I was being treated. A passing truck broke my fall and I survived, but a few weeks later, I was back on the same balcony, determined to finish the job. But then a strange thing happened. As I was standing there, preparing to jump—actually waiting for a break in the traffic—a news broadcast came on the radio about Vietnam and how hundreds of American GIs were now being killed every week. A mother who had lost both her sons in the space of a weekend spoke of their deaths. I'll never forget her voice. She talked as if her skin was on fire. The report said the average age of the dead now hovered at around nineteen. Still teenagers, still boys. Many were too young to have a damn beer, but old enough to die for their country. It suddenly occurred to me that suicide seemed like such an extravagant waste when young soldiers were being summarily wiped out in a country halfway across the world. That's when I decided to enlist."

"Well, considering the alternative, I'm glad you made it here."

Fletcher smiled and massaged the small of his back. "Try to get some rest, Trav."

"You, too," he said, then yawned like a man who hadn't truly slept in a very long time.

"Thanks, Fletch. I know how hard that must've been to talk about."

"That's the first time I've told anyone the story."

"I'm privileged, then."

Within a few minutes, Travis was fast asleep, most likely to dream about his own dead wife, Fletcher thought. Travis had lost his wife a year before coming to Vietnam. She was driving to work early one morning when a car skipped a traffic light and plowed into her. She was in a coma for over a month, but died the day after their wedding anniversary. Blood tests revealed that she was nine weeks pregnant—it would have been their first child. The driver of the other car wasn't drunk or driving recklessly, but had simply fallen asleep at the wheel after returning home from working night shift. The man had been pulling two jobs to keep his family from financial ruin. One night after a few beers, Travis spoke of how difficult it was to mourn the loss of his wife when he couldn't direct his anger at anyone. The man who took her from him seemed a good husband and father who was simply pushing himself into an early grave for his family. Travis never filed any charges and, over time, was even able to forgive the man.

While Travis slept, Fletcher removed his friend's glasses and placed them in his top pocket. He leaned forward and folded his arms on the edge of the foxhole. The sun was a harsh red, a fiery mirage on the horizon. In a short while, it would be dark. Vietnam sunsets were beautiful while they lasted, but gave way to sudden darkness—there was little honeymoon between day and night, and the soldiers dreaded the night. They were at their most vulnerable under the cover of darkness, partly because of the enemy's tactics of striking in the early-morning hours, but also because it was the one time when soldiers were truly alone with their thoughts and fears. Still, Fletcher savored the sunset, which at this time of year, was something of a rarity to witness. Most late afternoons were accompanied by heavy showers, the kind of incessant rain that, regardless of your shelter, would permeate your clothing like damp rising up a wall and leave you itchy and uncomfortable for the rest of the night.

Grateful for the respite, Fletcher scanned the dense jungle that spread out below them. Years of war had taken their toll on the vegetation, and large clearings were visible in areas that had sustained heavy bombings. But the jungle was recovering. New shoots and foliage thrived on the edges of bomb craters. Large trees had been felled, but new ones were already competing to take their place. He wished all wounds could heal so easily. As the last of the day's sunlight disappeared over the edge of the earth and the insects' nocturnal song intensified, Fletcher could feel the jungle's heartbeat. It pumped with as much life as it did death.

Four

By midmorning, Gunther had confirmed their coordinates via radio and ordered their pickup within the half hour. Other choppers would follow to secure and develop the area, but their job, at least for the meantime, was over. Squad leader Wayville Rex and Kingston Lane, whose intensely dark complexions and large frames suggested a familial resemblance where there was none, were instructed to set up three separate smoke canisters in the jungle surrounding the landing zone that would be deployed once the helicopter was within range. Each canister contained a different color smoke. The pilot would then have three potential pickup points, of which only one was correct. Gunther would reveal which one they were positioned next to only at the last available moment. If Charlie was nearby, he would have to guess their location and, consequently, the pickup zone. The helicopter would swoop down and hover just above the ground as the men clambered on board. This was by far the most vulnerable time of the operation. Scores of helicopters had been brought down by rocket launchers as they waited either to pick up soldiers or drop them off. Fletcher found it remarkable that despite many U.S. UH-1 helicopters being shot down, a surprising number would be retrieved by larger helicopters known as Chinooks and Skycranes. The Hueys would be repaired and sent back into action only days later.

Waiting anxiously, the Fat Lady listened for signs that its lift was approaching. As usual, Mitchell was the first to hear it. "Flapping bird. Flying from the east."

Rogan bided his time before giving the instruction to deploy the canisters. As the helicopter's drone grew louder, he gave the order.

Ribbons of red, blue, and white smoke billowed into the sky.

The command of red was given to the pilot in a simple code. It was something of an inside joke, as the Fat Lady only ever waited under red smoke. Within seconds, the Huey swooped down over the trees. It was coming in so fast, its tail rotor clipped the branch of a small tree.

Rogan gritted his teeth. "Fucking cowboys."

The Fat Lady hurried toward the chopper and scrambled on board. As always, Rogan was at the rear, looking for any signs of activity in the trees behind them. He turned around for the last few yards and launched himself up into the cabin. He raised his hand, extended his index finger, and swung his wrist around in a circular motion, signaling the pilot to fly. His hand was still turning when something caught his attention.

A flash, a puff of smoke, and a series of drowned-out hollow thuds.

"*Shooter!* Shooter at one o'clock!" he shouted, immediately returning fire. Mitchell, Travis, and Wayville quickly joined in. They sprayed hundreds of rounds into the trees until they were out of range.

"Fucking gooks!" Mitchell yelled out into the jungle, before hawking up the phlegm in his throat and spitting it out the door.

"Is everyone all right?" Rogan asked.

"We're cool . . . we're cool," Travis replied, "but Gunther's going to need a new radio."

"What?" Gunther frowned, removing the radio from his back.

Smoke wafted out from a burnt hole in the middle of the pack.

"Son of a bitch! I knew there was a reason I signed up for comms!" He bent over and kissed the scorched canvas.

"If you buy it a drink, maybe it'll give you a blow job." Wayville smiled.

"Real funny," Gunther smirked. "Real fucking funny."

Five

The Strip, as it was known by the soldiers, was located thirty kilometers north of Dak To in a highly mountainous area near the Laos border. Situated on top of a hill, it was classified as a small base—little bigger than a firebase—home only to some six hundred troops. It contained the usual spattering of tents and prefab buildings, several munitions stores, bunkers, watchtowers, a mess, and, of course, base headquarters. It was surrounded by thick, rusting reams of barbed wire and further protected by mines linked to large oil drums brimming with a lethal combination of diesel and napalm. If Charlie wanted to get up close and personal with them, he would first have to tiptoe his way through the Strip's tricky dance floor.

Despite its size, the base was in perpetual motion. Like its namesake in Las Vegas, the Strip never slept. It was one of the few bases still operating at full capacity anywhere near the demilitarized zone.

Fletcher plodded toward the tent he shared with Travis and

Mitchell. Some time ago, there had been a fourth, an edgy farm boy from Kentucky named Hank Landolin, but he passed away from complications arising from malaria. Had he not died, the army might well have imprisoned him, as he had neglected to take the mandatory prophylactic medication that was provided to all U.S. soldiers. It was a deliberate oversight on Hank's end. Contracting malaria was one of the many ways soldiers tried to get out of combat.

After removing his helmet, Fletcher slipped off his boots and settled into his stretcher. He made sure he was alone before pulling out a photograph he kept folded in his back pocket. As he straightened its corners, his breath caught in his throat. It never failed to move him. The picture was of his wife and daughter, taken in their sitting room almost a year before the crash. The camera that captured it had a self-timer that allowed him to be included in the photograph. However, in his haste to get into place alongside his girls, he had slipped on the rug and fallen headfirst into the couch. Scrambling to his feet, he literally dived in front of the lens at the last moment. When the photograph was developed, he couldn't believe how well the image had come out. It showed Abigail and Kelly in hysterics, watching wide-eyed as he lunged comically across the bottom half of the frame. They looked so happy, so perfect; it was an image that inadvertently captured their essence. Abigail, with her long black hair and sultry blue eyes, and Kelly, with a thick mop of mahogany hair and bright green eyes, were incandescent on the small square of film.

It reminded him of all the wonderful times they had shared—many of which he had taken for granted. If only he had known they were living on borrowed time, he would have made more of their days together. He would have spent fewer hours at work and invested less energy in things that didn't matter. He would have held hands for longer. He would have pushed Kelly on her swing until it was dark.

He would have slept less and lived a good deal more. But most of all, he would've told them both how much he cherished them every single day.

He stared at the photo for as long as he could bear before slipping it back into his pocket.

Six

That night, like most evenings after an excursion, the Fat Lady gathered at the Soup to blow off some steam. The pub was little more than an old tent furnished with a few tables and benches, a string of old Christmas lights draped from the roof, and a dilapidated fridge that frequently threatened to expire but so far continued to keep their beers cold.

Although the tone of their conversation was jovial enough, Fletcher sensed there was something bubbling beneath the surface. Wayville, in particular, had the look of a man who wanted to get something off his chest. "Hey, Wayville," Fletcher said, flipping the crown off a fresh beer. "Who pissed in your bed? What's on your mind?"

"This war is what's on my mind," he replied, staring down into his glass. "Christ, am I the only one who sees that we're getting our asses kicked out there?"

"Easy," Mitchell warned, his eyes barely slits in the soft light. "Leave it alone."

"No, screw it! We're getting fucking slaughtered out there! Every day we get weaker, and the gooks keep advancing. We're losing this goddamn war. I want to know when it's going to stop. When will there be enough rotting body bags before those cunts in Washington finally pull the plug on this bullshit? How many men have we lost? Fifty thousand? More?"

"Don't do this to yourself," Travis said. "We all know it's bullshit, but this kind of talk will drive you insane."

"So, are we just supposed to sit back and take it? I'm sick to hell of—"

"Of what?" Rogan interrupted. He was standing at the entrance to the Soup. "Finish your sentence, Rex."

Wayville paused, then lowered his voice a notch. "C'mon, Lieutenant, our missions are a waste of time. We're risking our necks, and for what? To delay the inevitable? How many troops have already returned home? The war will soon be over."

"You don't know that."

"Maybe not, but I sure as fuck don't want to get my ass shot off while the politicians try to figure out how we can get out of this mess with our pride intact."

"Whether or not the war is drawing to an end cannot factor into your thinking. Let me make this very clear to all of you: We're all part of a bigger machine. Our job is to keep our heads down and execute our orders. End of story. I shouldn't have to paint you a picture, but if Lord's mind begins to wander while he's at point and he starts contemplating his place in the universe, we die. If Pearson radios in the wrong coordinates for support fire, we die. If Green decides not to be a medic, but instead to scratch his dick and wonder how many days he has left in this shithole, we die. And if we die," he said, slamming his fist into the table, "then the men behind us die! Do you get me, Rex?"

The room fell into a deep silence.

Rogan glared at each of the men, demanding their support.

Finally satisfied, he took a deep breath. "While you're all together, you may as well know we've got orders for a recon mission the day after tomorrow. We spread our wings early—two hours before first light." He scanned the room, waiting to be challenged. When no one spoke, he turned and walked away.

"What makes you so immune?" Wayville called out. "Why doesn't this shit get to you? You're like a . . . fucking empty shell!"

Rogan drew to a halt. Then, clenching his fists, he spun around and marched toward Wayville.

"Lieutenant," Gunther began, stepping in front of him, "he's had a few drinks. It's been a long day—"

"Move, Pearson."

Without breaking stride, Rogan pushed past Gunther, leaned forward, and punched Wayville in the middle of his chest. The force of the blow sent him sprawling backward over a table and into the side of the tent.

"You ever talk to me like that again, I will rip out your goddamn throat," he warned. This time, there was no reply.

Seven

For the first time that Fletcher could remember, the Fat Lady flew in total silence. Were it not for the sound of the helicopter's rotors cutting through the air and the wind swirling through the cabin, it would have been like sitting in a mausoleum.

They were headed to what was considered one of the most dangerous areas in Vietnam: Lao Trung. To make matters worse, it was a reconnaissance mission, where they would have no ground or air support. If they came under heavy fire, they would be alone. Their job was to establish the level of activity in the region and pinpoint Charlie strongholds. The coordinates would then be radioed back to base, and the various camps and compounds would later be bombed with daisy cutters.

To exacerbate the uncomfortable quiet, tension still lingered between Rogan and Wayville.

"It feels like we're chasing a runaway car off a cliff," Travis eventually said, keeping his voice down.

"Chasing? We're fucking strapped into the car . . . and it's on fire," Fletcher countered.

"Jesus, will someone please say something out loud," Gunther called out. His eyelids, which were seldom hoisted beyond half-mast, gave the impression that he was continually tired. This, coupled with a set of high-riding eyebrows—like the raised wheel arches of an old car—gave him an almost comical look.

"All right . . . you're an idiot," Kingston offered.

"And an ugly cunt," Wayville added.

A smile tugged at the corners of Gunther's mouth. "Screw you clowns! You boys should come spend a few days in my hometown—then we'll see how many jokes you'll be telling."

"The only time I'll come out to your piece-of-shit redneck town is to pick up your sister," Wayville taunted.

"You leave Janey right out of this. I don't even want you thinking about her!"

The rest of the men laughed, partly at the sudden high pitch in Gunther's voice. Jane Pearson was a beauty queen of some fame, and the men often gave Gunther a hard time about it.

"And that goes for the rest of you," he warned, unable to suppress a faint smirk. "That's my baby sister you're talking about."

"Hey, Gunther . . . did you ever . . . I mean, have you ever thought about—"

"You finish that sentence, Wayville, and, as big a motherfucker as you are, I'll shove this radio right up your ass!"

Even Rogan managed a smile at that, but it was short lived. Moments of levity in Vietnam seldom lasted.

They were approaching the drop-off zone.

Eight

Jump, land, roll, and run for cover—basic military training. What the army couldn't equip you for, Fletcher thought, was the sickening feeling that Charlie might be waiting behind you in the trees, his AK-47 trained on your back. It never failed to prick up the hairs on his neck. It was the kind of aching dread that would keep soldiers from their sleep both in Vietnam and, for those lucky enough to survive, during the nights that followed.

As Fletcher hit the ground, he rolled and tried to get onto his feet in one fluid motion, but slipped on a patch of gravel and fell onto his back. The weight of his pack pinned him briefly to the earth like an insect impaled on a thumbtack.

"Jesus, Carson, get on your feet!" Rogan yelled, grabbing him by his collar and wrenching him up.

Together they scrambled to a nearby rock. They all held their positions as the Huey climbed and disappeared over the treetops.

So far, so good.

The key now, Fletcher knew, was to get moving as quickly as possible. The helicopter would have alerted Charlie to their presence, and they would soon be scouring the area for them. As of now, they were being hunted.

Rogan quickly called everyone in. "Fallow, what business are we in?" He always asked the same question at the start of an operation.

"The business of survival, lieutenant."

"That's fucking right! Let's remember that. Think before you goddamn break wind. Everything you do here has a consequence. Get your minds focused." He hastily pulled out his map and compass and confirmed their route. A minute later, they were moving. For reasons of superstition more than anything else, they usually traveled in the same formation: Mitchell at point, followed by Rogan, Wayville, Gunther, Kingston, Fletcher, and Travis. The three teenagers—Edgar Green, Craig Fallow, and Arnold Keens—always brought up the rear. Rogan insisted on it. Although he never offered an explanation, Fletcher knew why: The young men were a great deal safer at the back, shielded to a large degree from traps, ambushes, and even sniper fire.

Fletcher peered over his shoulder and could see the fear etched on each of their young faces; it was sheer madness that they had to share in the burden of another generation's war. Ironically, by Charlie's standards, these men were already senior citizens—some of their recruits were barely teenagers.

As Fletcher wondered again how a nation of fathers could send their children to war, and whether or not any of them would see nightfall, he scanned the dense jungle ahead of them.

They had almost thirty kilometers to hike.

Their day, like most in Vietnam, would be excruciatingly long.

Nine

By late morning, they had made good ground. Because of the meandering nature of the terrain, it was difficult to work out exactly how far they had traveled, but they had moved quickly, encountering nothing more sinister than the jungle's wildlife. Of some concern were three water buffalo they had stumbled onto a mile ago, drinking from a shallow river. The animals were known to be domesticated by the Vietcong, but after a brief sweep of the area, it was clear these three were on their own. The temperature had been hovering at around seventy-five degrees for much of the day, but the mercury now pushed up into the nineties. That, coupled with the stifling humidity, made it increasingly difficult for the platoon to maintain its concentration.

They had just stopped to eat and to tend to their blisters and insect bites when Mitchell raised his hand as a sign of danger. Back on the Strip, they had often joked that he was two parts bloodhound, one part human. But there was no laughter now.

Mitchell hesitated, as if reading subtle vibrations in the air, then pointed to a small hillock ahead of them. Without saying a word, he dropped down onto his stomach and began to crawl up the hill. Rogan and Fletcher followed behind him. Reaching the top, they carefully parted the tall grass, and Fletcher eased his rifle through the gap.

There were four men, moving slowly, less than two hundred yards away.

"What're they holding?" Fletcher whispered, squinting.

Rogan reached for his binoculars. "Bow and arrow . . . and a spear . . . they're hunting." He panned the binoculars away from the men and saw what they were after. "Wild pig."

"Are the men soldiers?" Fletcher asked.

"Looks like . . . Montagnards."

"What?"

"Jungle people," Mitchell replied. "Hunters. Not many of them left. Some believe they're also cannibals."

Fletcher watched as the four distant shadows closed in on their prey. With unnerving precision, the man in front drove a long spear into the animal's back. The pig squealed briefly, then fell silent.

"All right, no need to sound the alarm. Let's just get moving," Rogan decided.

They retreated quietly down the embankment, collected their gear, and moved out. After a few minutes, Fletcher pulled up alongside Mitchell. "Those men were almost two hundred yards away. How the hell did you hear them?"

"I didn't. I could smell shit in the breeze. When animal crap is that strong in the wind, it's normally because it's been smeared on something; in this case, the Montagnards. They were stinking out the place."

The jungle was a bouquet of different smells, including plants, herbs, dead animals, rotting leaves, mud—not to mention a wide variety of excrement—yet Mitchell had still managed to discern that something was amiss. "Unbelievable."

"It's because he used to sleep out in the barn back home," Wayville commented from behind, casually chewing on a strip of sugarcane.

Mitchell didn't take the bait; he never did out in the field.

"You could learn a lot from Lord," Rogan said without looking back. "Like how to stay focused and concentrated."

Wayville rolled his eyes, but said nothing. He knew better than to argue the point.

Three hours later, they were nearing the area where they planned to hole up for the night, when Mitchell stopped walking in midstride. He lowered down onto his haunches and inspected the path ahead of him. It was covered with thick banana leaves. He carefully pried them up.

Rogan knelt down beside him. "What've you got?"

"Possible soldiers on a skewer."

The leaves had disguised one of Charlie's most devastating traps: a Punji pit. Sharpened bamboo sticks like snake's teeth lined a deep cavity in the ground. The rest of the platoon quickly gathered around.

"That's the first one I've ever seen," Arnold Keens said, his voice tinged with awe.

"Me, too," Craig Fallow added.

Mitchell shook his head. "Something's wrong."

"What is it?"

"Too easy . . . they wanted us to find it. They used banana leaves. Proper Punji pits are covered with mud, small leaves, and bits of roots. They wanted us to find this, but why—?"

"Stop!" Rogan suddenly called out to Arnold Keens, who had wandered around the side of the pit to get a better view. "Do not move." He walked over to the young infantryman and knelt down. He gently pressed on the innocuous-looking foliage at his feet. The ground immediately caved in, revealing a second Punji pit. This was the one intended for them. It was twice the size of its counterpart.

Arnold slowly stepped back. "Christ, that was close."

Enraged, Rogan leapt to his feet. "Keens! Who told you to break formation? Since when do you move ahead of point?"

"Sorry, Lieut—"

He grabbed the youngster by his collar and, without realizing it, lifted him clean off the ground. "You need to think more about what you're doing! We're in the land of the devil, and he's a cunning son of a bitch. Do you understand?"

"Yes . . . sorry, sir."

"What are we in the business of?"

"Survival, sir."

"What was that?"

"Survival, sir!"

Instead of releasing the young man, he pulled him closer. "Arnold, I'm tired of writing letters to mothers explaining how their sons died."

"I'm sorry, sir. It won't happen again, sir."

"It better not," he replied, letting him go. "It better not."

It was the first time Fletcher could ever remember the lieutenant calling one of them by his first name. *Perhaps he's human after all,* he thought.

Ten

Another night in hell, another hastily dug foxhole.

Travis had managed to fall asleep with relative ease, but Fletcher was again left grappling with the oppressively dark night. Wary of evening patrols in the area, they had set up camp halfway up an embankment under heavy vegetation. Instead of the infinitely glittering night sky above them, they had banana leaves and thick palms, like the overlapping hands of giant men, as their heavens.

For his earlier lapse, Arnold Keens and his foxhole-mate Edgar Green were pulling watch between 0200 and 0430. Fletcher listened as the two soldiers quietly discussed topics natural to men of their age. They spoke intermittently about cars, music, and surfing, but their conversation inevitably gravitated back toward women, or more specifically, the prostitutes scouring the shores of China Beach. They both had some time off due to them and were planning to spend it getting blind drunk and losing themselves in the comforting folds of

Vietnam's thriving skin trade. Although most of the men were involved in relationships with local women—sordid or otherwise—it bothered Fletcher that so many children were being born who would never know their fathers. He tried to imagine a life in which he would turn his back on Kelly, but couldn't.

After a while, he tuned out their conversation and turned to his own thoughts. The prospect of the war coming to an end left him feeling conflicted. He was genuinely happy that American troops would soon be able to go home to their families and return to the lives they had left behind, but he felt for the South Vietnamese. Without support, they would succumb to the North within a matter of weeks. They would no more be able to hold them back than they would a tidal wave. Once their defenses were breached, they would be overcome and then punished for siding with the enemy. Of that, he was certain.

The end of the war would, once again, leave him adrift. The jungles of Vietnam had neither claimed him nor provided him with renewed purpose. All the war had done was darken the nightmares that plagued his nights and wore away at what remained of his sanity. If by chance he made it out, what would he do with the rest of his life? Return to Chicago? Not likely. He doubted he would be able to face anything that resembled his earlier life. He would have to relocate. Change jobs. Meet new people. Try to outrun his past. If he couldn't, there was always a comforting balcony he could revisit. Sometimes he could feel it calling out to him. Like something from a sinister fairy tale, it seemed to possess a kind of supernatural attraction. It was the gnarled hand of a hooded stranger offering candy to a child.

Increasingly, he was tempted by its pull.

Fletcher woke up to the sound of rain pelting down on the leaves overhead. The drops were sporadic at first, but soon chorused into a torrential downpour.

"Just a week without getting wet, that's all I ask," Travis said, his eyes still closed. "Tell me I'm dreaming the rain."

Their hooch was covering their bodies well enough, but water was pouring down the sides of the pit.

"You're dreaming the rain."

"Tell me the Cubs won the World Series."

"Sorry, but even dreams have a toehold in reality."

Travis sat up and wiped his face, which was partially spattered with mud. "What's the time?"

"Almost 0430."

"Shit. It feels like I just closed my eyes."

"It'll be light soon."

"Then what? We all drive to a bar and have a few beers? Maybe a couple of steaks?"

"Something like that. Instead of going to a bar, though, we'll hike for another ten hours through the inside of a furnace, trying gamely not to get our asses blown off, and instead of steak, we'll have a couple of the shittiest biscuits known to mankind," Fletcher replied. "Speaking of which, want one?"

Travis was not yet prepared to surrender the fantasy. "Make my steak rare, very rare. In fact, just swat the cow over the head with a newspaper."

"And to drink?"

"Bourbon. You can leave the bottle."

A gust of wind shifted the rain, slanting it against their backs. "Jesus. If we're not dying of heat, we're being lined up for pneumonia."

"It could be worse," Fletcher observed, gagging on the first half of his biscuit. "The Cubs could actually have won the Series."

Travis smiled and rubbed his eyes. "Did you get any sleep?"

"About an hour, if you count all the blinking."

"That's pretty good for you."

"Yeah, but I'm thinking of giving it up altogether. Every time I fall asleep, I keep waking up in Vietnam."

"I know what you mean. I have the same dream."

Fletcher paused, then adopted a serious tone. "What are you going to do with your life when you get out of here?"

"Don't you mean *if*?"

"Humor me, Trav."

"I'm not sure. No long-term plans, really, apart from maybe bombing Washington. But I do know the first thing I'm going to do."

"What's that?"

"Fly to Miami. Book into a hotel with clean, crisp white sheets and a view of the beach. I'll spend my mornings swimming in the ocean and my afternoons watching it from my balcony. At night, I'll let the tides lull me to sleep."

"And the seagulls will wake you in the morning?"

"Absolutely."

"Sounds like a postcard."

"It's not too much to ask, is it? A piece of happiness."

Fletcher smiled warmly. He could imagine Travis sitting on a balcony with a drink in his hand, gazing out over an azure ocean. The image seemed to fit like an old wristwatch.

"What about you?"

For a while, he was quiet. "Go visit my girls. Tell them about this place. Remind them how much I miss them."

"And after that?"

"Who knows? Maybe I'll fly out to Miami. Spend some time with a friend."

"I do need someone to mix my drinks."

Given their situation, the very thought of wading out into the Atlantic seemed surreal to Fletcher.

"It keeps me going, you know," Travis said, watching muddy water pool at their feet. "When this place gets to me, it's all I think about. Come with me, Fletch. We'll stay a couple of weeks, then figure out the rest of our lives."

Outside their foxhole, the jungle was now a solid gray sheet of rain. "What? And give up all this?"

Eleven

Four days later, the Fat Lady was finally on its way to the extraction point. Drained both physically and mentally, they had gathered all the information they required and plotted the coordinates of numerous enemy bunkers, hooches concealing munitions and food supplies, at least half a dozen field bases, and a bridge that, once taken out, would seriously hamper the NVA's supply line. Fletcher was startled at just how quickly Charlie was advancing and how strong he had become. He was on the ascendancy, dramatically so, and they all knew it. Despite his thousands of dead, the war was his to win. All they could do now was try to slow him down.

They had narrowly missed being intercepted by NVA patrols and had twice been forced to separate. In the end, they had conducted most of their forays in two squads: one headed by Rogan and the other by Wayville, who, before being assigned to the Fat Lady, was a fully fledged operational squad leader.

With only two kilometers left to hike, the men were quiet. Having survived a week in the enemy's basement, they were anxious for fresh air. Mitchell, still at point, was completely wired and absolutely focused. He appeared determined not to let his guard down. He seemed to regard Charlie's traps not so much as weapons of war, but more as personal affronts. He would shuffle forward a few steps, then stop, breathe deeply, scan the area in front of him, and then dart forward again. Sometimes he would rub his hands on the ground and lick the tips of his fingers. Fletcher wondered, with genuine concern, how he would ever adapt back to normal life.

As was typical toward the end of an assignment, Rogan dropped to the back of the platoon to shepherd his men from the rear. Within a matter of hours, their entire area of operations would be the subject of an intense bombing campaign. Most of the men they had stolen past, laughing and drinking cheap alcohol outside huts and bunkers, would soon either be dead or wishing they were. The thing about war is that you could be on the winning side before breakfast, but still be dead by nightfall.

The thought brought no joy to Fletcher.

"Halt!"

"What is it?" Kingston asked.

Mitchell shook his head as if his eyes were deceiving him. "A dog."

Fletcher turned to his right. In the distance, a yellow Labrador with its tongue lolling out the side of its mouth emerged from between the trees. The animal was moving badly, favoring its left side. What appeared to be a large cut ran from the top of its back down its front leg. Flies, like a black mist, hung over the wound. More disturbing, though, was a swollen mass of what looked like dried blood caked under its neck. "What the hell is a dog doing out here? Christ, look at him."

Rogan briefly studied the animal, then gestured to Fletcher. "Take him out."

"What?"

"You heard me, Carson."

Fletcher was taken aback by the order. He watched as the dog slipped on the wet undergrowth and then struggled to get back up. He looked weak and hungry. "What are you talking about?"

"Are you deaf? Kill the fucking dog, that's an order. There's something around its neck, probably a mine."

Fletcher raised his rifle and looked through the scope. "It's just blood and dirt."

"This isn't a debate. Take the shot."

Fletcher followed the animal in his sights as it approached them. In his first days in Vietnam, he'd spent some time at a base that had a dog unit attached to it. All the animals there had been German shepherds, but he had heard that there were many Labradors working as scout dogs throughout Vietnam, trained to provide early warning of enemy patrols, ambushes, mines, and traps. "I'm not doing it. There's no danger."

Rogan placed his palm over the top of his sidearm, but kept it holstered. "Take the shot."

"You first," Fletcher said, glancing down at the lieutenant's hand.

"What the fuck is wrong with you? It's just a goddamn dog!"

"He's one of ours. The only Labradors in Vietnam belong to us. He must've got separated from his handler. He's a soldier, for Christ's sake! Besides," he bargained, "if I shoot, we'll reveal our position—"

"I'm warning you. This is your last chance."

"I'm not doing it."

The Labrador was less than a hundred yards away and closing.

"Keens . . . take the shot," Rogan instructed.

Arnold Keens, who'd been watching their exchange in disbelief, recoiled at the sound of his name.

"Your rifle, Keens! That metal thing strapped around your skinny neck. Use it! Take out the dog."

"C'mon, lieutenant you can't expect Arnold—"

"Shut up, Tucker."

"But, lieutenant, I . . . I can't. Wh-what—"

"Fire your weapon, son!"

Reluctantly, Arnold raised his gun and took aim.

"Don't do it, Arnold. Let him come to us. He's hurt. He recognizes our uniforms. He's one of us. There's no danger—"

"Shut your mouth, Carson."

Fletcher turned to face the teenager. "Arnold, look at me. Please, don't shoot him."

"Discharge your weapon, or I'll have you thrown in prison!"

Fletcher locked eyes with the young man and immediately realized he'd lost him. Arnold was scared to death and did not have the resolve to defy a direct order. *Sorry, Fletcher,* he mouthed.

The Labrador, sensing that something was wrong, stopped walking.

"Forgive me," Arnold whispered, and squeezed off two rounds.

The first shot punched into the dog's chest, and the second into the top of his front leg.

He collapsed onto his side and immediately tried to stand up, but his legs buckled under him. The wound in his chest, just below his head, was oozing thick black blood. Confused, he looked down and began to lick at the holes that were hurting him.

Something unraveled in Fletcher's mind. He threw off his pack and launched himself at Rogan.

"Fletcher, no!" Travis yelled, scrambling toward them.

A look of surprise lit up Rogan's face. Before anyone could

intervene, Fletcher lowered his shoulder and hit him in the stomach. The force of the blow lifted him off his feet and sent him hurtling into a tree. Fletcher charged after him and started swinging his fists wildly, connecting with his face and chest. "You fuck!"

Wayville and Kingston quickly pulled Fletcher away. A thin rivulet of blood flowed from Rogan's nose. "Have you lost your goddamn mind, Carson?"

Fletcher didn't reply. He couldn't. His mind was teetering on the edge of a breakdown. He had rarely felt such anger, such hatred. He turned away and ran toward the dog.

"No," Gunther warned. "There could be traps."

But his words were lost to the jungle. Fletcher could think only of getting to the animal's side. As he passed Arnold, the young man held up his arm. "I'm sorry, Fletcher. Please . . . I'm so sorry."

Fletcher struck out at his hand as if it was poisonous to the touch. "Fuck off."

By the time he reached the dog, it was clear he was dying. His chest was heaving in an irregular motion. Blood from his wounds had formed a half moon around his body. There was blood, along with other fluids, draining from his nose. Kneeling down, Fletcher carefully placed his hand on the Labrador's side to try to comfort him. As he touched his coat, the dog lifted his head and looked at him. Instead of fear, his eyes conveyed a look of sadness, a glimmer of betrayal. Fletcher felt his stomach tighten. "You were coming to us for help, weren't you?"

The dog tried to lick his hand, but was slipping away.

Fletcher gently stroked the side of his face. "I'm so sorry, boy."

Then, steeling himself, he withdrew his sidearm. With his hand shaking and his vision blurred with emotion, he took aim. "Close your eyes."

The Labrador looked first at the gun and then back at him. Slowly, his tail swept across the ground.

"No," Fletcher pleaded, biting down on his lip hard enough to draw blood. "Please." He was about to pull the trigger when he heard a voice over his shoulder.

"Don't do it," Travis said softly, pushing the top of the gun down with his hand. "He deserves a chance to live."

Twelve

Fletcher carried the critically wounded Labrador all the way to the pickup point. He should have weighed around sixty or even seventy pounds, but in his malnourished state was little more than half that. Edgar, their medic, had applied tourniquets to both wounds, but he continued to lose blood and was drifting in and out of consciousness. As they waited for the chopper to arrive, Fletcher tried to funnel water into his mouth, but the dog could barely swallow. Long strings of saliva hung from his jowls. "C'mon, friend . . . just a few sips."

The dog looked at him, blinked, then closed his eyes. For a moment, Fletcher thought he was gone, but his chest continued to rise and fall in an uneven rhythm.

He was hanging on, but only just.

Sitting opposite Fletcher, Travis gently patted the side of the dog's face. "He's going to make it. I just know it. There's something about him."

Fletcher nodded, but couldn't bring himself to reply. Something deep within him had given way, and he couldn't clearly understand it. Watching the dog being shot had triggered an all-consuming, almost pathological rage. He knew his actions would have severe repercussions when they returned to base: There would be a hearing, and he would most likely be court-martialed and imprisoned. But none of that mattered now. All that concerned him was trying to save the dog.

Edgar knelt down beside the Labrador and listened to his chest. "Look I can't be sure, but I think one of his lungs is punctured."

"Will he make it back to base?" Fletcher whispered.

"His wounds are very serious."

"Will he make it back?"

"We have no idea how much internal bleeding there is or which organs have been damaged."

"You aren't answering my question."

Edgar continued to examine the dog. "No, I'm not."

The next few minutes limped by. They were about to be extracted from the most demanding assignment they had ever been on, but the scent of death still hung over them. Partly out of concern and partly to run down the wait, the men all spent some time at Fletcher's side. However, wary of their actions being interpreted as support for his insubordination, most of them did not stay long. Only Travis and Edgar remained with him.

"Bruno Ship," Fletcher announced.

"Who?" Travis asked.

"Bruno Ship. He's a chef in the Officers' Mess."

"Yeah . . . bald guy. Friendly. What about him?"

"A few weeks ago, we got to talking. It turns out he ran out of money and had to drop out of vet school in his final year."

"Vet school? You sure?"

"Yeah. He'll help us. He'll operate on the dog."

"Fletcher," Edgar said. "I don't think I need to state the obvious here, but you're up to your neck in shit. The army's going to come down hard on you for what you've done. I'm not sure Bruno is going to want to have anything to do with this."

"He'll help, I know it. I've heard him talk about his dogs back home. But I need you to do something for me."

"What?"

"We need to get the dog into the hospital as quickly as possible."

"No way. There's far too much activity there, trust me. Your best bet is to set something up in one of the tents."

Fletcher thought for a moment. "Okay, but what about supplies?"

"That I can help you with."

"All right, then. As soon as we get back, you're going to have to source whatever you think we might need."

"It shouldn't be a problem. I have a key to the supply room. No one keeps a real inventory, anyway."

"I'll help you," Travis offered.

"Thanks, but if someone sees you, they'll suspect something's up. It'll be safer if I do it on my own."

Fletcher looked down at the Labrador and gently traced his fingers down the length of his nose. Each ragged breath seemed certain to be his last. "Hold on, boy, hold on."

In the distance, the sound of rotor blades whooped toward them.

Thirteen

"Shit!" Bruno Ship deliberated, scratching the stubble under his chin. He was standing at the entrance to Fletcher's tent, where the dog lay sprawled out on a stretcher. "I've got only six weeks of this fuckfest left."

Fletcher nodded. "You're right. It's unfair of me to ask. If we get caught, it'll mean trouble for you."

"You're not making much of a case."

"I'm not trying to force this on you. There's a lot at stake, and I don't want to talk you into doing something you'll regret."

"It gets worse. I hope you weren't a salesman before the war."

"Look, I'll understand either way."

Bruno massaged his temples as if trying to ward off sleep. "In high school, I got one of the highest grade-point averages in the whole of Detroit. I had six universities offer me full scholarships. I could've studied to become a neurosurgeon if I wanted to, but I chose veterinary science. Do you know why?"

Fletcher shook his head.

"Because I've been trying to save animals since I was four years old. Of course I'll help."

Fletcher felt his throat tighten. "Thank you. I really appreciate it. Once the operation's over, no one will know that you were ever involved. You have my word on that."

"If the army is going to make an example out of us for trying to save a defenseless animal's life—possibly one of its own scout dogs, no less—then forgive my manners, but the army can go fuck itself. As it is, I'm not too pleased with the institution. Most of my friends are in the habit of not returning from their little picnics in the jungle."

Fletcher was buoyed by Bruno's attitude. "Okay, when do you want to operate? Tonight?"

"No. Edgar was right. Our friend has punctured a lung, and there's a lot of internal bleeding. We need to drain the chest cavity and do what we can to repair the damage."

"Now?"

Bruno shook his head. "As in half an hour ago."

Fourteen

Bruno quickly compiled a list of medical supplies he needed and handed it to Edgar to source. He then instructed Fletcher and Travis to boil two large pots of water and find a new mosquito net under which he would perform the operation. To make the environment as sterile as possible, the net would be doused in disinfectant.

"I've got a net I've never used," a voice said, drifting into the room. "It's yours if you want it."

It was Mitchell, and he wasn't alone. Wayville, Kingston, Gunther, and Craig Fallow were standing alongside him. "What can we do to help?"

Fletcher raised his hands. "Thanks, guys, but there're enough people in the firing line as it is."

"Fuck that. What can we do?" Wayville insisted.

"I appreciate the offer, really, but there's nothing else for you to do.

Bruno has agreed to perform the operation, and Edgar's organizing the supplies. But I will take you up on that mosquito net, Mitch."

"Done."

"How's he doing?" Kingston asked, moving over to the stretcher.

"He's holding on, but not by much."

"If he survives, we'll make him our mascot."

Fletcher nodded, but knew that if the dog somehow did recover, he would soon be reunited with his unit. After all, he was probably carrying lice and other germs that the base commander would not take kindly to.

"How long do you think you've got before they haul you down to HQ?" Wayville asked.

"Hopefully long enough to get the tent set up for the operation."

"Do you think it's wise having it in your tent? This is the first place they'll come looking for you."

"No, you're probably right, but I can't get anyone else involved now. It has to be here. That is—" He paused, realizing he hadn't consulted the tent's remaining occupant. "—if you don't mind, Mitch?"

"My castle is your castle."

"Why don't you use our tent?" Kingston offered. "We have a spare bunk as it is."

"Thank you, but as I said, there are already enough people at risk."

"What're they going do to us? Send us to war?"

"They could lock you up."

"Clean sheets . . . three meals a day . . . no gooks . . . yeah, that's a real nightmare," Gunther replied.

"Look . . . if you're all that bent on helping, I suppose there are a few things you could do."

After a brief discussion, the men quickly set about their various tasks. Mitchell and Wayville would station themselves outside the tent and turn away anyone who came looking for Fletcher, while

Gunther and Kingston got on the radio to try to find out where the closest dog unit was. If the Labrador made it through the operation, they would need the unit's help with food and medicine.

Fletcher and Travis were about to douse the mosquito net with disinfectant, when they noticed Arnold Keens sitting on his own. He had the look of a man at conflict with himself.

"I've got this," Travis whispered. "Go talk to him."

Fifteen

"Arnold, are you all right?"

The infantryman, transfixed in another world, flinched as Fletcher's shadow was cast over him. "Fletcher . . . I'm so sorry. This is all my fault," he blurted out, his eyes red and swollen.

"No. It's me who owes you an apology. You have nothing to be sorry for. You were given a direct order, and you obeyed it. You were right to do what you did. I'm an asshole for trying to make you disobey your commanding officer."

A sob, the kind often produced by young children or men at war, racked through Arnold's body.

"Arnold, listen to me: I'm the one to blame here. What I did placed the entire platoon at risk. I wasn't thinking clearly."

"Why did the lieutenant order the shot?"

"He thought the dog was a threat to us."

"But there wasn't any danger."

"It doesn't matter now. He must've had his reasons."

"What's going to happen to you?"

"I'm not sure, but they'll be coming for me."

"Why don't we go speak to the lieutenant, we could—"

Fletcher held up his hand. "Thank you, but no. I'll face up to whatever's coming my way."

They were quiet for a while as Arnold tried to collect himself. "How's he doing? Is he going to make it?"

"I don't know, but a few good people are pulling for him. That's got to make a difference, don't you think?"

"I hope so," he replied, dry-washing his hands. "Why'd you make a stand, Fletcher? Why risk yourself?"

"I don't know, really. I can't explain it. I just felt a connection to him. I imagined he'd been lost in the jungle for days—wounded, starving, trying to find his handlers, and there we were . . . his salvation. He recognized our uniforms. He was coming to us for help, and we were going to kill him. I just couldn't allow it."

"I wish I had your courage."

"Don't confuse what I did with courage."

"I don't think I am."

A jeep roared past them, spewing up a cloud of dust and grass in its wake.

"Do you know if he's one of ours?"

"I haven't noticed any markings to confirm it, but I'm pretty sure he is. I can't think of any other explanation for him roaming around the jungle."

"He's lucky to have had you in his corner. If I haven't killed him, the bombs would've done the job in the morning."

"You haven't killed him. He's got a fighting chance now that Bruno's agreed to operate."

"Let me do something, please, Fletcher. Let me help."

"Well . . . there's so many people involved now, what's another name on my conscience?"

Arnold smiled appreciatively. "Sometimes I think there's just too much to take out here. Too much shit to get your head around."

"You think that only sometimes? This is hell on earth, Arnold."

"Yeah," he agreed. "The people back home . . . they'll never understand what happened here."

"True. But the good news is that it will all be over soon. You've just got to hang in there. You'll be back with your family before you know it."

"Thanks, Fletcher. Christ, I can't wait to go home. See my brother, my parents . . . my girl. I'm sure you must be missing your family?"

Fletcher nodded, the light fading from his eyes. "You could say that."

Sixteen

I'm ready," Bruno announced, snapping on a pair of latex gloves. He was standing in front of the tent that was now a makeshift surgery.

"All right," Fletcher sighed, scanning the area for any signs of his imminent arrest. "You sure you want to go through with this?"

"Uh-huh."

"What about you, Edgar? You don't mind assisting?"

"You couldn't drag me away."

"Enough chat, gentlemen," Bruno cut in, stepping backward into the tent. "Let's get moving."

"Good luck," Fletcher offered, walking away.

"Where're you going?" Mitchell asked, shaving the side of his arm with his hunting knife.

"To the Soup."

"Why?"

"To hide out for a while, buy some time. I'll lose my mind if I wait around here."

"Want some company?" Wayville asked.

Fletcher thought about it for a moment, then looked at Mitchell. "All right with you, my Lord?"

"Of course."

"What if someone comes looking for me and insists on checking the tent?"

"Well," Mitchell replied, and held up his knife. "I can be quite persuasive."

"Still not incarcerated, I see," Kingston joked, entering the Soup. He was followed by Gunther and the diminutive figure of Craig Fallow.

Fletcher was sitting at a table with Wayville and Travis. "Not yet, but it shouldn't be long now."

"Well, they sure are taking their sweet time."

"I'm trying not to think about it. Have either of you been past the tent? Are they still operating?"

"Yeah, they're still working on the slug in his chest. They haven't even got to the one in his leg yet."

"Christ, it's taking forever."

"Relax, Fletch," Gunther said. "Maybe this'll cheer you up: I got hold of a dog unit in Dak To. Their squad leader is willing to help and has set aside medicine, food, and dips for our patient. They've promised to keep it quiet."

Fletcher's expression brightened. "That's great, but how're we going to get it here?"

"Remember our pilot friend we rescued?" Craig asked. "The good Will Peterson? Well, as Lady Karma would have it, he's now based in Dak To and has changed shifts with one of his buddies to run the stuff over to us this afternoon. They're loading up the supplies as we speak."

Fletcher was visibly moved by the news. "I don't know what to say."

"Hey, this isn't your personal crusade." Wayville held up his arms, his immense frame casting a wide shadow as he stood up. His eyes, set deep within his skull, glowed like two small lanterns left under a large outcrop of rock. "None of us wanted to see the dog shot in the first place. You just showed more balls than the rest of us."

Kingston, himself only a shade smaller than Wayville, but several years his senior, removed his jacket and slung it over his shoulder. "That was some gutsy shit you pulled out there."

"Nothing gutsy about it. I just saw the dog coming toward us, needing help, and we were going to shoot him. It just didn't seem right to me."

"At one point, I thought Rogan was going to tear your arms off."

"If you guys hadn't separated us, he probably would've."

"You didn't do too badly. We were all quite surprised at how well you fared."

"Not bad for a pretty boy," Wayville added.

Fletcher allowed himself a wry smile. "The lieutenant's not the bad guy in this. He was just trying to protect us."

Gunther clapped loudly. "That's very charitable of you. I doubt Rogan's returning the favor right now."

"What's your argument going to be when they eventually come and get you?"

"I don't know. I suppose I'll just say that I was wrong. Out of line. That I endangered the safety of the platoon."

"Jesus Christ, do you want to get yourself thrown in prison?"

"I don't really care to be honest."

"How's Arnold doing?" Kingston asked.

"I had a chat with him. He feels really bad about his part in all of this. In fact, he's shattered by it."

"Poor kid."

"I think he'll be all right, though. I explained that he was right to follow orders, and I apologized for what I did. Craig . . . the two of you are good friends," he said, looking up. "Will you watch him for me?"

"Sure. Will do."

Gunther pulled out a chair and sat down. His short blond hair and reddish beard glistened in the morning light. "I think the only reason Rogan was so determined to have the dog taken out was because of how hard-assed you were being. That's the first time I've ever seen someone stand up to him. Was probably a fucking first for him, as well."

"I don't know—"

"Carson," a voice suddenly called out. Three armed soldiers were standing outside the entrance to the Soup.

"Just on cue, gentlemen," Fletcher replied cynically. "I don't suppose you want a beer?"

Seventeen

Fletcher was escorted not to base headquarters as he had expected, but to the officers' pub known as the Tip. Inside, the prefab was deserted save for a single patron occupying the table next to the bar. Having delivered Fletcher, the three officers turned around and quickly strode away. Rogan was nursing what looked like a glass of water, his index finger circling the lip of the tumbler. As Fletcher approached him, he tried to study his face, to get a sense of where the lieutenant's mind was. There was definitely still some anger in his eyes, but there was now something else there, as well. Something he couldn't read.

"Do you know why they call this place the Tip?" Rogan asked, keeping his head bowed.

"No, sir."

"I've heard one of the men say it's because officers arrogantly think they're more important than the men who serve under them.

The old 'tip of the spear' bravado bit—that without the edge of the blade, the rest of the spear is useless."

Fletcher nodded, but said nothing.

"It's called the Tip because you can pick up valuable advice in here that might save you and your men out there," he said abruptly, shifting his stare to the prefab's solitary window.

Realizing that whatever was about to come was not part of a formal procedure, Fletcher pulled out a chair and sat down.

"Do you know how long I've been in Vietnam? This is my third tour. It's been almost three years. Two of that as lieutenant. Seen a lot of death on both sides. I've witnessed great acts of bravery, but mostly just scared young men doing whatever they can to stay alive. Most of them couldn't give a flying fuck about the politics that keep us here. Most came because they had no choice, or wanted to prove a point to their fathers. I read that in World War Two, only one in four soldiers fired his gun during combat; in fact, in the First World War, the majority of soldiers died of flu. The point is that most of our men out here are terrified and will do whatever they can to get back home in one piece."

The Tip's barman appeared over Fletcher's shoulder and placed a beer down in front of him. Things were not progressing as Fletcher had anticipated.

"But the Fat Lady is different. To a man, I have witnessed exceptional courage. We might have our ups and downs, but everyone genuinely looks out for one another. The Fat Lady is something special. Something rare."

"I agree."

"Then explain something to me: Why did you choose to threaten what we have today? What made you decide to jeopardize all that we are?"

"I don't know what came over me. I just couldn't let the dog die."

"Do you think I wanted to give the order? Do you even understand why I did it?"

"Yes, because Charlie has been known to booby-trap animals with grenades and mines," Fletcher replied. "But there was nothing tied around his neck, I told you—"

"Not *around* his neck, Carson!" Rogan shouted. "Inside it! They stitch handmade bombs no bigger than your fist into the loose skin under their necks. The bombs blow the animal to pieces and send a cloud of napalm fifty feet into the air. I know! I've watched it happen."

Fletcher sat upright in his chair, sweat now prickling through the skin on his arms and neck. He thought back to how the dog's neck was caked in blood. "Christ, lieutenant, I didn't know. I'm sorry—"

"Fuck sorry. *Fuck it!*" he yelled, grabbing his glass and hurling it across the room. "You could've killed us. Besides that, the dog looked fucking rabid. I should've shot you today. What you did was selfish, stupid, and put everyone's lives in danger. Do you really think I wanted to have the dog shot? *Jesus!*"

Fletcher closed his eyes. He was at a loss for words.

"I know why you're here, Carson. I know what happened to your family, and I'm sorry for what you've been through. But that doesn't give you the right to impose your death wish on the men you serve with. I've watched you in combat. You display the kind of fearlessness that only a man who has nothing to lose can show. Up until now, it's made you a highly effective soldier, but today it could've cost us our lives. I can't have you on board unless you get your head on straight."

"You're right," Fletcher replied, holding up his hands. "Please believe me; I never meant to endanger the men."

Rogan looked up at the ceiling, but did not reply.

For a while they sat in silence.

"What happens now? When is the hearing?"

"There isn't going to be one. The Fat Lady shovels her own shit."

"Are you telling me I'm not going to be formally charged?"

"Not officially, but I want you to apologize to the men. Especially Keens. God knows why, but that boy looks up to you, and you put him in a very difficult position today."

"I've already spoken to him. I feel terrible about it."

"What I have to know right now is," Rogan carried on, leaning forward, "are you a liability to us? Can I expect any more bullshit from you?"

"No, sir. You have my word. I won't go against your orders again."

Rogan took a deep breath. "All right, that's it. This is over. Get out of here."

Fletcher hesitated for a moment before lifting to his feet and heading toward the door.

"Carson, wait. How's the dog doing?"

"They're still operating."

"*Operating?* Who is—?" he replied, and then shook his head. "Never mind."

Eighteen

As Fletcher left the Tip and made his way past the munitions store, he began to truly comprehend just how reckless he had been. He shuddered at his selfish behavior and knew that in time he would have to find a way to make amends with the men whose lives he had jeopardized. But that time was not now. Running, he cut in front of a jeep and turned toward his tent. Mitchell was still guarding the entrance. "How's he doing?" he asked, trying to keep his voice down.

"Your timing's perfect—they've just finished."

Bruno stepped out of the tent, wiping his bloody hands with a towel.

"Bruno . . . how'd it go?"

"We pulled out four slugs. Two of ours, and two AK-47 rounds. Our two were in the chest and front leg. Theirs were in the back leg and neck. I'm not going to lie to you, Fletcher, he's lost a lot of blood—maybe a fifth of his body weight."

"What're his chances?"

"Two, maybe three out of ten at a push. Given the nature of the operation and our lack of proper disinfectants, dressings, and the right antibiotics, our biggest enemy now is infection. In this climate, it's going to be a hell of a job to keep his wounds dry and healthy."

"How much damage did the bullets do?"

"There's significant muscle and tissue damage. He's got three cracked ribs, a punctured lung, and his front right leg was partially dislocated. The bullet that punctured his lung also nicked his liver, which caused serious bleeding."

Bruno saw the disappointment in Fletcher's face. "Look, the round in his neck was a ricochet. It's only a soft tissue wound. I think his legs will recover. My real concern is his breathing and whether or not we've stopped the internal bleeding. If he makes it through the next two or three days, I'm going to have to open him up again. One of the problems with dogs is that they're so eager to please us that they seldom give us a real indication of how they are healing. Often they'll get hit by a car, run home, and act like nothing's happened—only to drop dead an hour later. I'll have to go back in and check for myself."

"So what do we do now?"

"We wait. Gunther tells me the proper antibiotics will be here shortly. The sooner I can administer those, the better. We've got him on a drip, and his breathing is still ragged, but it has stabilized."

Edgar pushed through the flap guarding the entrance to the tent and shielded his eyes from the bright sunlight. "This man is a genius. He did a great job. He's given our boy a fighting chance."

Fletcher, swallowing hard, thanked both men again and headed into the tent. Mitchell followed closely behind.

The mosquito net, draped over the stretcher, gave the room a clinical feel. The smell of disinfectant was almost asphyxiating.

"Let me," Mitchell said, lifting up the damp netting.

The Labrador's coat, which had been caked in mud and dry blood, was now clean and golden, save for the white dressings on his legs, neck, and chest. The loose skin on his face folded up around his eyes in thick, silky wrinkles. His breathing was still labored, but it was better than before.

"Bruno says we have to turn him once at night and twice during the day."

Fletcher knelt down next to the dog. He gently placed his hand on the side of his nose. A wave of affection swept through him. He had felt an almost otherworldly connection to him right from the start. Inexplicably, he felt as though he knew the dog—that somehow they had crossed paths before. That somehow this animal was no stranger to him.

As he stroked the side of the Lab's face, Mitchell spoke. "I can't help but notice that you're not in chains."

"Rogan's not taking it any further. He had words with me, but that's it."

"You're off the hook?"

"Apparently."

"What'd he say to you?"

Fletcher briefly took him through their conversation. "I owe everyone an apology. I'll speak to the men tonight. Rogan and I might not get along, but he was right about today."

Mitchell wiped a thin veneer of sweat from his forehead. "You were both right."

Suddenly there was a commotion outside. The tent flap parted, and in stepped Travis and Gunther, carrying boxes of medical supplies.

"That must be a world record," Fletcher said.

Travis placed one of the boxes down and pulled out a letter. "This is for you."

Fletcher quickly unfolded the note and read it out loud:

Dear Corporal Carson,

Your man has told us about your predicament and what you are doing to try to save the life of what you believe is a U.S. scout dog.

Look inside either of his ears, and there should be a letter and number marking his unit. Once you find it, radio the information back to me, and I'll trace where the dog comes from. If he recovers, we can arrange to get him sent back to his handlers.

No doubt, there will be serious repercussions for your actions, but as squad leader for our dog unit, I must thank you for what you are doing to save the life of one of our own. Our dogs are saving hundreds of soldiers' lives and are helping to keep us in this war, but they're not getting the credit they deserve.

Within these boxes, you will find all the medicine we own and some the army doesn't even know about. It comes with our thoughts and prayers.

We hope it makes the difference.

Let us know if there is anything else we can do to help you.

Sincerely,
W. Wallace
Squad Leader, Wolf Pack

Alongside his name was a stamp of a German shepherd sitting at its handler's feet. The words IN DOG WE TRUST underlined the image.

Nineteen

That night, while Travis and Mitchell slept, Fletcher shifted his stretcher up alongside the dog. He listened intently as the animal drew one strained breath after another. He was worried that if he fell asleep, he would wake up to find the Labrador dead. So, despite his exhaustion, he remained awake, reaching under the net to stroke the dog's chest every few minutes. His touch seemed to have a soothing effect, or so he liked to believe. Two drips, both half-empty, hung from the top of the tent. The life-giving fluids were fighting infection and keeping him hydrated.

"How's our patient?" Bruno asked, entering the tent holding a small plastic box.

"What're you doing here?"

"Couldn't sleep, worried about our boy. I see I'm not alone on that score."

"What's in the box?"

"Change of dressings, disinfectant, and a thermometer. I want to see if his temperature has come down at all."

"He's doing all right, but he's battling to breathe again."

Using Fletcher's torch, they quietly changed his dressings and were surprised to discover that his temperature had dropped by almost two degrees.

"That's encouraging; it means the treatment's working," Bruno remarked. He dropped to his haunches and gently lifted the animal's jowls to inspect the color of his gums. Satisfied, he then pulled down one of his eyelids to look at the tissue lining.

Fletcher took a deep breath. "How're things really looking?"

"Honestly? I didn't think he'd survive the operation. The fact that his blood pressure is strong and his temperature is coming down are all very good signs. It's better than we could've hoped for."

"But?"

"Listening to his chest, it's not good. If he makes it through the night, I'm going to have to open him up sooner than I thought."

Fletcher nodded slowly. "Have you ever seen a dog make it through worse?"

"Dogs are amazing creatures, especially Labradors. You'll be amazed at what they can endure. He's got the spirit for a fight—I can feel it."

"I hope you're right."

Bruno looked up at Fletcher and removed his glasses. "If I may ask, why are you so attached to this dog?"

"I've been asking myself the same question, but I'm still no closer to an answer," Fletcher replied. "He can't die, Bruno."

"Then we won't let him," he said solemnly. "Now get some rest."

Twenty

Travis wiped the sleep from his eyes. "Jesus," he said, yawning. "Tell me you got some rest last night?"

"Slept like a baby," Fletcher replied.

"Liar," Mitchell whispered, sitting up. "How's he doing?"

"Same as yesterday. Just holding on."

Both men stood up and walked over to the dog.

"Bruno was here early this morning to check on him. Apparently his circulation has improved and his temperature has come down, but . . ."

"It's his breathing," Mitchell said softly. "I can hear it."

"Bruno wants to operate again today. Doesn't think he'll make it otherwise."

Mitchell bent over and lifted the net. He knelt down and brought his face level to the dog's head. Taking great care, he parted the Labrador's eyelids.

"What're you doing?"

"I've seen a lot of dead eyes in my time. In the heads of the dead and the dying. You can tell when someone's about to go. The light . . . it fades," he said, as if he were privy to a more profound understanding of mortality. "Our friend isn't ready to go. Not for a while."

"Morning all," Bruno said, cradling supplies in his arms. "I take it our boy made it through the early morning?"

"I didn't think he would a few hours ago, but he's still with us."

Bruno fished out his stethoscope and placed it on the Labrador's chest. He immediately frowned. "Fletcher, what're your duties this morning?"

"Nothing, we're off for another two days. Why?"

"I need an assistant."

"When?"

"Right now. We have to operate immediately. He's drowning in his own blood."

"What about Edgar?" Travis asked, preempting Fletcher's question.

"He's assisting in an amputation."

"Are you sure I can help?"

"I am. Besides, he's your dog now, and if he's going to leave us, you should be here with him."

"All right," Fletcher said, clearing his throat. "What do I do?"

"How long has it been?" Wayville asked, sitting on a patch of grass outside the tent.

"Almost an hour and a half," Travis replied.

"Should it be taking this long?"

"How the hell should I know?"

"Arnold, you had extensive medical training, didn't you?"

"Just the basic shit. CPR, how to apply tourniquets, stitching . . . crap like that, but I have no idea how long an operation of this kind should take."

Kingston stood up and stretched. "Let's take a look-see at what's going on."

"Yeah, why not?" Wayville agreed, and quietly lifted the tent's flap.

They all adjusted their positions to get a better look inside. The smell of ammonia wafted out to them. It was so powerful, they had to close their eyes for a second to allow the outside air to dilute it. Beyond the mosquito net, Bruno was hunched over the dog. Fletcher, standing alongside him, was holding a clamp that disappeared deep into the dog's abdomen. They were both concentrating intensely.

"Can we get you guys anything?" Gunther asked, breaking the silence.

Neither man replied; they seemed oblivious of the question.

"Let's leave them be," Mitchell said, closing the flap. "If they need our help, they'll ask for it." He turned away and was about to sit back down . . . when the first mortar hit.

Twenty-one

Incoming!" a panicked voice issued from the base's northern watchtower.

"No shit!" Gunther yelled, feeling his face for shrapnel.

Wayville instinctively reached for his gun. "Anyone hurt?"

Travis's glasses had shielded his eyes from the dust, and he was able to scan the area. "I don't think so."

"How the fuck did Charlie get so close? It's broad daylight, for Christ's sake!"

Soldiers, half-dressed, some busy shaving, spilled out of their tents.

Officers barked orders. Jeeps roared to life. Pilots ran for their choppers.

Another mortar whined toward them.

"Get down!" Kingston shouted.

The missile hit less than fifty yards away from them, taking out a small prefab supply hold. Running with their hands over their heads, three uniformed soldiers charged toward an unmanned gun battery.

Another mortar hit, farther away this time.

Then another.

The base took close to a dozen hits before it answered with heavy artillery fire. Giant howitzer rounds mowed through the jungle beyond the clearing, felling large trees as if they were hollow beneath their bark. Two Phantom helicopters swooped overhead, immediately laying down rocket fire in the cover beyond the base.

Another mortar hit, flipping an unmanned jeep onto its side.

Mitchell, seemingly unaffected by the chaos, stood up and stared out into the jungle.

"What are you doing? Get down, Mitch!" Wayville said, covering his ears.

Mitchell breathed in the caustic smell of cordite. His eyes focused on a distant hillside some four hundred yards away. "Show yourself, ghost," he whispered. His eye caught a flash of steel and a puff of smoke. "I see you . . ."

He immediately ran toward the nearest gun battery. The soldier manning it was firing wildly into the air. "Move," he commanded.

The soldier was visibly relieved to relinquish control. Mitchell spun the field gun around and opened fire. The ground shook as the giant rounds tore into a concentrated area on the hillside.

Travis crawled up to the tent and threw up the flap. "Fletcher . . . Bruno, you've got to get to a bunker."

"We can't. If we leave now, he's dead."

"No, Bruno, Travis is right! Get out of here."

"No way. I'm not leaving."

"Bruno, you—"

"Fuck off!"

"Shit! Shit! Fletcher, what about you?"

Fletcher looked up and shook his head. By the expression on his face, Travis knew that a mortar itself would have trouble extricating him.

Suddenly three small holes punched through the side of the tent. Then another two.

"Jesus!" Travis yelled, diving down.

Both Bruno and Fletcher stood their ground.

"C'mon, Fletcher, this is fucking crazy!"

"If I let go of this clamp, he'll bleed out. I'm not moving. Now, get out of here."

Gunther, lying behind Travis, tugged at his pants. "I've got an idea." He pointed to an armored vehicle parked opposite them. "It'll shield them."

Travis's eyes widened in agreement.

Together, they ran to the vehicle as puffs of dust exploded at their feet. *Please let the keys be in the ignition,* Travis thought as Gunther leapt into the cabin and reached under the steering wheel. The distinctive jangle of metal sent a wave of relief pulsing through him. Gunther twisted the key and slammed the truck into gear. Moments later, the vehicle skidded to a halt in front of the tent.

"Are you guys all right in there?" Travis yelled.

For a moment, there was no reply; then Bruno swore. "Damn it . . . we're losing him."

Twenty-two

Within minutes, the attack was over. By the time the helicopters had emptied the last of their cannons, it was clear Charlie was gone. A sweep revealed shells and blood at half a dozen sites, suggesting the offensive might have involved as many as fifty soldiers, but they found only two bodies. Once again, the ghost had managed to carry most of his dead and maimed away with him.

All told, the Strip lost four jeeps, two Hueys, an entire gun battery on the eastern perimeter, a supply compound, and, the worst of it, twelve men. A further six were seriously injured. Despite everything, Bruno and Fletcher had managed to complete the operation. At the height of the mayhem, the Labrador's blood pressure had dropped alarmingly, but they managed to stabilize it.

Of the dozen dead, only one was really known to Fletcher. James Kent was a friendly and likable soldier who was part of a logistics company that played a low-key though vital role in the war. His nickname was Teddy Bear because of his chubby face and disarming smile. Fletcher imagined his passing would sadden scores of people both on the base and back in his hometown. To the American government, however, he was just another cataloged casualty, a number in a body bag. Another letter to be posted.

Sitting outside their tent as the sun dipped over the trees, Fletcher, Bruno, and Travis were nursing a few cold beers. They had spent the afternoon towing away debris, leveling areas where the mortars had hit, and even helping to find and bag body parts.

"How'd they get so damn close?" Travis asked.

"I think the real question is *why,*" Fletcher countered. "They had no real hope of taking out the base. As soon as the first mortar hit, they would've known they'd come under heavy fire. Why do it?"

"To fuck with us. To send us a message," Bruno said. "That they can hurt us whenever they want."

"Just a quick twist of the knife and then gone . . . into the fucking ether," Travis added, running his hands through his thinning hair.

"You have to give it to Charlie, though—he is one gutsy, conniving bastard," Fletcher remarked, knowing that in the wrong company, his comment would spark outrage.

"In the end, it all comes down to motivation," Bruno replied. "Most of us are here because we have to be. Our boys don't believe in the bureaucracy. All they want to do is get back home, preferably with most of their limbs still attached. Charlie is fighting for his way of life, for his survival. He would much rather die than have to march to our tune."

"Can you blame him?" Fletcher asked. "How would you feel if this was your backyard?"

"I don't know, but speaking of backyards . . . I sure as hell miss mine."

Travis drained the last of his drink. "What really bothers me is that, just like Wayville said, we're in this void at the moment where everything we do is meaningless. It's one thing risking your neck when there's a purpose to it, but it's something else when you know that no matter what you do, the outcome has already been decided. The men who were killed today . . . died for nothing."

Neither of the men challenged Travis's statement. They both knew it was true; for all intents and purposes, the war was already over.

For a long while, they sat in silence, listening to the sounds of the night, until Fletcher finally spoke. "Why'd you carry on, Bruno?"

"I'm sorry?"

"Why'd you go through with the operation?"

"It just felt like the right thing to do. If we'd stopped and abandoned him, he would've died. It seems to me that too many people have invested too much in him for me to just give up when things got a little hairy. Why'd you stay?"

Fletcher shrugged. "I had nowhere to be just then."

Travis shook his head. "You're both out of your fucking minds."

Fletcher handed out another round of beers. "A toast, gentlemen. To friends coming together to help one another. And to those among us who commandeer armored vehicles to protect a crazed surgeon and his deranged nurse."

Fletcher and Bruno both raised their drinks to Travis. "Despite everything," Fletcher declared, "some things are still worth fighting for."

Twenty-three

During the next two weeks, the Fat Lady was involved in a company-sized foray into the mountains of the Central Highlands near the Cambodian border. Not for the first time, they operated at point with Mitchell effectively leading a team of three hundred men on another seemingly futile exercise through the sticky mess of Vietnam. During nine days, they were involved in two firefights. Their exchanges claimed thirty-four Vietcong, but they suffered heavy losses of their own; eighteen U.S. soldiers would never see their families again. The Fat Lady, however, had emerged intact.

By the time the helicopters arrived to pick them up, Fletcher was becoming increasingly anxious. He was desperate to find out how the dog was doing. In the days following the operation, the Labrador's vital signs had shown dramatic improvement. His temperature had dropped to within the normal range, there was a steady rhythm to his breathing, and, most important, it appeared as though he had fought off earlier signs of infection. But still he remained in a coma.

The flight back lasted three quarters of an hour. When they eventually touched down, he jumped from the helicopter and ran for his tent. Many of the men he sped past regarded him suspiciously—soldiers hardly ever ran on base unless there was an emergency. As he made it to the tent, Bruno emerged, wiping the back of his neck with a towel. His friend's expression told him most of what he needed to know.

The news was not good.

"He's alive, but I'm afraid he's in a deep coma. He hasn't regained consciousness since you left."

Fletcher let his pack drop to the ground; his chest was heaving from the run. "What does this mean?"

"I'm sorry, Fletch. If he hasn't regained consciousness now, there's a good chance he may never do so."

Fletcher made no attempt to hide his disappointment.

"I'm afraid the bad news doesn't end there. Wilson has found out about all this, and he's not pleased. He wants you, Travis, and Mitchell in his office first thing tomorrow morning. Evidently he's not aware of my role in the proceedings."

"And that's how it'll stay."

Despite feeling responsible for implicating Travis and Mitchell, Fletcher didn't care much what Battalion Commander Frank Wilson thought or planned to do. Few punishments carried more threat than remaining a soldier in Vietnam. "Thank you for everything."

Bruno nodded and placed his hand on Fletcher's shoulder before stepping aside.

As Fletcher moved into the tent, he was stunned by what he saw. Letters and cards of goodwill covered the inside walls of the tent. On the canvas wall to his right, pinned to the material, were hundreds of dollar bills placed next to each other like tiles. There had to be three or four hundred dollars' worth.

"What is this?"

Bruno shuffled past him and pulled off one of the crumpled bills. "Read for yourself," he said, offering it to Fletcher.

Scribbled in red ink near the top of the bill was the message: *Fletcher, consider this the Strip's contribution to helping you save your dog. Good luck.*

"There's been something of an outpouring of support while you've been away. It started the day after you left, when three of the soldiers approached me and asked if they could see the dog. At first I denied any knowledge, but after they told me that most of the base knew what was going on, I let them in. They stayed at the dog's side for hours, offering to help in whatever way they could. The next day, there were ten soldiers. The day after that, thirty."

Fletcher pulled off another note and read the message: *It was either this or more cigarettes. And you know how much I love my coffin nails.* It was signed José Alvares, the Soup's part-time barkeep.

Overwhelmed, Fletcher moved away from the money wall and turned his attention to the dog. The mosquito net was still draped over his stretcher. Lifting the gauze, he sat down next to the Labrador. The animal's golden coat seemed to have brightened since he had last seen him. From the look of it, he had put on at least four or five pounds.

"He looks so good," Fletcher said, battling to keep his emotions in check. "He just needs to wake up." He placed his hand on the dog's flank and lightly stroked his fur. Running his fingers up his body, he rested his palm against the dog's nose. It felt warm and moist. "How've you been managing with the drips?"

"I was close to running out after the first week, but one call to our benefactor, and another consignment was with us the next morning."

"He's a good man."

"We have enough drips for another five days or so, and the men's donations should keep us going with whatever else we need for some time to come. It's all up to him now."

Mindful of exposing the animal to whatever he might've picked up during the past few days, Fletcher stepped back and pulled down the mosquito net behind him. Again, he surveyed the walls of the tent. "I can't believe this. I never knew we had so many animal lovers."

"I'm not sure we do. I think it's more a case of what our patient represents. Most of the men associate dogs with their lives back home. It gives them something familiar to cling to. Something normal."

"Either way, I'm grateful for their support," Fletcher said, reading the message on another bill. "I just hope it's not in vain."

Twenty-four

Fletcher lifted Kelly above his head and threw her into an approaching wave.

She shrieked with delight, thrashing her arms around wildly. “Again!” she cried, wiping the salt water from her eyes. “Again!”

Fletcher grabbed her by her shoulders and again pitched her into an oncoming swell. She emerged laughing, her long hair plastered to the sides of her face.

“Easy, honey,” Abigail warned, joining them in the waist-high water. “That’s precious cargo you’ve got there.”

“Yes, Daddy!” Kelly agreed. “I’m very precious, don’t you know.”

“Precious? More like *precocious*!”

“*Pre*-what?”

“*Precocious*. It means ‘fish food.’ ”

Kelly slapped her hands on her hips indignantly, her pink bathing suit shimmering in the bright morning sun. “I’m not fish food.

I'm a princess—" she began, before a small but powerful wave knocked her off her feet. Most children would've burst into tears at the fright of being barreled over by the ocean, but not Kelly. By the time Fletcher had fished her out of the water, she was laughing again.

"All right, young lady." Abigail smiled. "That's enough for now. Let's go get something to eat, and we can come back later this afternoon."

Kelly's expression soured. She considered complaining, but then eased at the prospect of ice cream. "Can I have a bubble gum milk shake?"

"Okay, but then no dessert."

Kelly mulled over the deal for a moment. "Then I'll have to have a big one . . ."

Fletcher shook his head. "She's going to make us truckloads of money one day as a bloodthirsty attorney."

"C'mon, let's go," Abigail said, reaching for Kelly's hand. Fletcher, in turn, took Kelly's other hand, and together they waded out toward the beach. As they trudged forward, Fletcher noticed that the underwater currents had grown stronger since they first entered the water. As he pushed on, leaning forward, he seemed to step into a hole, and the water leapt up to his chest. Instinctively, he held Kelly back.

"That's strange," Abigail said. "This wasn't here before."

"We must've stepped off a shelf. Let's try a different route to the beach."

Fletcher also noticed that the sky overhead, which he was certain had been clear only minutes before, was now heavily overcast. A wind rose up and sprayed sea salt in their eyes.

"What's going on?" Abigail asked, raising her voice above a sudden crack of lightning.

"I don't know," Fletcher said, using all his strength to fight the ocean's pull.

"The current's so strong. We're going to be sucked out to sea!"

"Don't panic," he replied, but his words were lost to a gale that now blasted across the choppy water.

"Daddy, don't let us drown!" Kelly pleaded, squeezing his hand.

Fletcher looked back over his shoulder, then down at the water around them. What was a deep cobalt blue before, was now a thick and morose black, a massive expanse of ink. He spun around again, searching for the sanctity of the beach, but it was no longer there.

"Somebody help us!" Abigail cried, now treading water and clinging desperately to her daughter. Kelly, in turn, began to scream.

With his free hand, Fletcher wiped his eyes and again searched for the beach. It was nowhere, seemingly consumed by the alien ocean. The soft sand underfoot was also lost.

The wind cut up the water's surface, and between swollen thunderheads, more lightning fired synapse-like on the horizon. Then came the rain. A fiery shower that burnt like acid as it pelted down on them. Where it greeted the water, it burst into streaks of ruby flame.

And then his girls were gone.

The current that he'd been fighting so hard to resist tore them away from him and sucked them out into the bowels of the ocean. Their bodies moved at an impossible speed. He swam out frantically toward them, but they soon disappeared.

The ocean, now a swirling mass of lava, began to pull him under.

As the fiery lip of a wave broke over him, his final words were lost to the hellish storm.

Fletcher woke with a pinched-off scream. The dream was exactly the same each time. Equally vivid and harrowing, but new to him on each occasion, a dream without an imprint in his memory. It had been a while since the nightmare had last played out in his sleep. *Hello, darkness, my old friend,* he thought morbidly to himself.

He sat up and used his sheet to wipe away the sweat on his face. As he tried to gather his thoughts, he felt a strange weight pressing down on his right thigh. He opened his eyes and looked down at the bed. The dog, lying alongside him, was resting its head on his leg. Fletcher swallowed heavily. He eased himself down the stretcher and leaned over the animal. Gently, he rubbed the side of the Labrador's face. His heart, still racing after the dream, began to pound even harder. He cleared his throat and spoke quietly. "Are you awake?"

The dog stirred, but remained unconscious.

Fletcher leaned in closer and repeated himself. This time the dog's ears pricked up at the sound of his voice. His jowls twitched, and his front right leg gave a short kick. And then, miraculously, he opened his eyes.

Fletcher felt a surge of warmth rise up in his chest.

The dog's rich brown and yellow eyes held Fletcher's stare.

"I never doubted you for a minute," he managed. "What took you so long?"

Twenty-five

I'll be damned," Bruno repeated for the third time in as many minutes. "I truly thought we'd lost him."

"We should have," Fletcher suggested, gently massaging the Labrador's neck. "But you saved him."

"I'm not sure how much I had to do with it. His injuries were very serious. Too serious, maybe."

"What do you mean?" Wayville asked.

"I don't know, really, but I think we had some . . . higher help. This dog was meant to survive."

"C'mon, that's bullshit."

"Is it? Do you have any idea how much blood he lost? Medically, it was virtually impossible for him to remain alive. Believe me, we're in the league of miracles here."

Seemingly aware that he was the subject of their conversation, the dog lifted his head and tried to sit up.

"Easy, buddy," Fletcher warned, helping to prop him up.

The dog looked down at the gauze patches on his body, then back up at Fletcher. His eyes were heavy with sleep.

"You're going to be just fine."

He blinked and then nuzzled the side of Fletcher's arm.

Arnold, who had been chronically depressed since the shooting, knelt down next to the Labrador. The dog turned, regarded him wearily for a moment, and then licked his hand.

Fletcher watched as the tears instantly welled up in the young soldier's eyes. In a single stroke, he had been absolved of his offenses. His relief was palpable. The group remained quiet, respecting the weight of the moment.

After a while, Gunther screwed open his flask and poured some water into an upturned helmet. "Let's see if he's ready to drink yet."

At first, the dog seemed uninterested, but his ears soon pricked up as if he suddenly remembered how thirsty he was. He quickly lapped up the water, splashing it all over Fletcher's legs.

Before he could finish, Bruno withdrew the helmet. "That's enough for now."

Travis moved toward the dog. "It's so strange that he's a Labrador. Most of the dogs I've seen out here are German shepherds."

"There're quite a few Labradors operating as scout and tracker dogs. They're very intelligent. Mostly used for picking up enemy tracks and providing early warning of snipers, ambushes, and traps. If he has training, we could actually use him," Mitchell replied.

As the possibility rattled around in Fletcher's mind, Bruno asked a question that was so startlingly obvious, he couldn't believe he hadn't thought of it before. "What're we going to call him?"

The question was clearly directed at Fletcher; the dog's name was his to give.

No sooner had the words left Bruno's mouth, than Fletcher had the answer. "Jack. We'll call him Jack."

"That was quick. Why Jack?" Bruno asked.

"I don't know." Fletcher shrugged. "The name just came to me."

Mitchell lowered down onto his haunches and cupped his hand over the side of the Labrador's face. "Well, Jack . . . welcome back to hell."

Twenty-six

Huddled together, nursing hangovers, Fletcher, Travis, and Mitchell waited to be summoned into Frank Wilson's office. The night before had been spent vigorously celebrating Jack's recovery.

"What's our plan?" Travis asked, more out of concern for his headache than from fear of being overheard.

"Let's request a dishonorable discharge from the war," Mitchell volunteered, his eyelids at half-mast. He hardly ever drank, but when he did, he really committed himself to it.

"Just leave the talking to me. It's my fault that you're both here."

"If you think we're going to sit back and let you play the martyr, you can forget it." Travis yawned. "Besides, what's the worst they can do? Send us to bed without supper?"

"This might be more serious than you think. Wilson might've found out about my fight with Rogan."

"Oh, yes . . . *that.*" Mitchell laughed. "Hell, that was entertaining."

"Hold on, Fletch, you told us you'd already spoken to Rogan and there wasn't going to be an investigation."

"He might've changed his mind."

"Rogan is full of shit, we all know it, but his word is good. If he told you there isn't going to be an investigation, he won't backpedal now."

Fletcher was about to respond, when the door to Frank Wilson's office opened. "Inside, gentlemen. Now."

"Sit down," Frank Wilson said in a tone that suggested it was not a request. He rolled up a large map of Southern Vietnam he'd been studying. "I suppose you know why you're here?"

"Yes, sir," Fletcher replied. "First of all, I want you to know that neither of these men—"

Frank held up his hand. "I don't want to hear it, Carson. Rogan has told me everything. I know that you men found the dog while on tour. I know it was Rogan's idea to bring him back and that you were just acting under orders, but I must tell you I'm not happy with the situation at all. Carrying an injured animal around on a patrol is both dangerous and stupid. Quite frankly, I was surprised by your lieutenant's poor judgment. But be that as it may, we now have to deal with the situation. I've been told that the dog has been under your care and that he regained consciousness yesterday morning. Is this true?"

Fletcher could not believe what he was hearing. Not only had Rogan covered up their altercation, but he had also taken the blame for Jack being brought to base. Fletcher felt a sudden, almost overwhelming sense of gratitude toward him, and in that moment, every preconceived notion he had of the lieutenant was cast into doubt. "Uh . . . yes sir."

"Well? Is he going to live?"

Sensing Fletcher had been put off his stride, Travis intercepted the question. "We hope so, sir. He's lost a lot of weight and he's very weak, but he's eating and drinking well now."

"I've heard about your tent, gentlemen. I've also noticed what his presence has done for the men. I won't deny that I'm moved by all the support your patient has had, but I have a base to run. I have to make sure that every decision we make is in the best interests of our efforts here. Have you checked the dog for any type of identification? We need to get him back to his unit if he's one of ours."

"We have, sir. All U.S. dogs serving in Vietnam are supposed to have coding inside their ears," Travis replied.

"And?"

"Well, there's nothing, sir. But we'll check again."

Frank sat back in his chair and folded his arms. "All right, gentlemen, seeing that you've taken an active interest in this dog, what is your recommendation?"

Fletcher, having regained his composure, recognized his opportunity. "I suggest we keep him here until he is fully rehabilitated."

"And then?"

"Then, sir, let's see if he has any training. We could use a dog here to patrol the perimeter."

"We don't have any facilities to care for dogs here. They need special food, medicine, dips—"

"Sir, we are fortunate enough to have been given the support of a nearby dog unit, who've provided us with supplies. We have all that we need at the moment. The men have agreed to personally sponsor whatever else we might require."

"You're the senior man in all of this, Lord. What do you make of this?"

"I think the dog has brought the men together and is doing

wonders for morale. And, to be honest, I think the base can do with all the good feeling we can muster at the moment, because we're getting royally fucked over out there."

Frank turned in his chair and looked up at the ceiling. "I want a plan, Carson. On my desk by the end of today. Where he's going to sleep, a list of the supplies we still need, a schedule to get him moving again—everything."

"Yes, sir. Appreciate it, sir."

"Lord's right, Carson. It's about morale at this stage. I'm not blind to what goes on around here. I've seen what this dog has done for the men. All right . . . dismissed."

As they turned and headed for the door, Frank stopped them. "Carson, wait," he said, offering a wad of dollar bills. "For your . . . money wall."

Twenty-seven

The next six weeks were spent largely rehabilitating Jack. At first, his progress was painstakingly slow. After the first week, they suspected his legs were permanently damaged, as he could barely stand for more than a minute before collapsing. He was eating and drinking better than any dog living in the backyard of American suburbia, but his lack of mobility was a major concern. A few of the men suggested it was cruel to see him suffer and that perhaps he should be put out of his misery, although no one dared say anything directly to Fletcher, who would sooner step on a mine than consider euthanasia. Jack had shown remarkable powers of recovery, and he wasn't about to lose faith in him now.

That faith was repaid a few days later when Jack tentatively began to take his first steps. After that, his recovery accelerated dramatically. As the circulation in his legs improved, he quickly progressed to a sure-footed trot. A few weeks later, he was able to run freely. The miracle was almost complete. The men each took turns walking, feeding, and looking after him, but mostly only when Fletcher wasn't able to. The dog may have become the base's mascot to some degree, but there were no illusions as to whom he belonged. As time passed, Fletcher and the Labrador became virtually inseparable.

Despite further attempts to find out where Jack had come from, their efforts were unsuccessful. Gunther had spent hours tracking down other dog units in the region, but none of them reported a missing dog of Jack's description. More surprising was the discovery that he was highly trained. It first became apparent when he reacted to basic commands, but even more obvious one morning when he was taken on a patrol of the base's perimeter. Fletcher noticed a change in him the instant he put on his leash. Using the full length of the restraint, Jack quickly moved ahead of him, sniffing the ground and processing the immediate area. They had been walking for only a few seconds when Jack suddenly dropped down and began to make soft whimpering noises.

"What is it, Jack?" Fletcher asked, moving up alongside him.

A low growl issued from the back of Jack's throat. It was the first time Fletcher had witnessed any form of aggression from him. Not sure what to do, he gently placed his hand on top of his head to calm him, but the growl only intensified.

Suddenly Fletcher understood. Less than a yard ahead of them, buried halfway in the mud alongside the fence, was a live mortar that had failed to detonate. A remnant of the attack they had suffered several weeks before. "Jesus," he said. He tugged at Jack's leash, and the Labrador instantly relented and followed after him.

The mortar was later safely detonated, and the majority of Jack's detractors, if any remained, were silenced. Every morning after that, Fletcher and Jack patrolled the perimeter as part of their daily duties.

It wasn't long before Jack's other talents were discovered. They had received a handwritten booklet of basic dog commands that Squad Leader Wallace had compiled for them. It consisted of typical word and hand commands used out in the field. Jack knew every one of them, without exception. There could no longer be any doubt about his past.

They also discovered his affinity for water. Wherever there was some of it to be found, however meager, he would gravitate toward it. After heavy rains, he would find pools to roll around in. While patrolling the base, he would seek out muddy trails where there were clearly paths of surer footing to take. Their benefactor explained that the dogs were trained to do that to hide their scent. Fletcher had no doubt it was true, but was convinced Jack did it for pure enjoyment.

As the memory of his injuries faded, Jack's true personality began to emerge. He was surprisingly mischievous. He would steal food out of the men's rucksacks and chew holes in their boots. It soon became necessary to stow any items of value well out of Jack's reach. Before long, he was joining the men in the Soup at night, happily lapping up any beer that was offered to him. His relationship with all the men blossomed, and he quickly became an integral part of life on the Strip. In a matter of weeks, he had worked his way into the affections of all on base.

All but one.

Despite taking responsibility for Jack being brought back to base, Rogan seemed uninterested in the dog, merely tolerating him. Fletcher tried to thank him for what he had done, but Rogan stopped him in midsentence. It appeared that he cared no more for being thanked than he did about whether the dog lived or died. His thoughts were only ever on the war and the role the Fat Lady had to play within it. This, however, was of little consequence to Jack, who continually sought Rogan out, as if he sensed the lieutenant's indifference toward him. In meetings, he would often sit at his feet or bark at him from across the room, as if trying to chip away at the barrier between them. To the amusement of the platoon, he even offered Rogan his paw during an intense briefing session.

But it had little effect.

Rogan's mind was totally focused on the war: A war they were losing.

Twenty-eight

"This isn't a debate," Frank Wilson declared, wiping his brow with a handkerchief. "The dog is clearly highly trained and could save your asses out there."

"We're not a dog unit, Frank. This is ridiculous," Rogan snapped back. "We're not even sure if he's ever operated out in the field before. He could give away our position at a vital moment."

"Listen, the dog follows advanced voice and hand signals to the letter. Yesterday morning, the men gave me a demonstration of what he is capable of, and I've got to tell you, I am damn impressed by what I saw. For whatever reason, he seems to share half his brain with Carson."

"This is madness."

"No. *Madness* is being forced to send you up the Chi San trail. You're going to be moving through some of the most treacherous terrain this war has to offer. I don't need to tell you how many soldiers we've lost on this run."

"Lord is the best point man we have. You know how good he is. If anyone can get us through it, he can."

"I know how good Mitchell is. What if you lose him?"

"We won't."

"Enough," Frank said, holding up his hands. "As it is, this foray is one shade light of a suicide mission. The dog could well make the difference. My decision is made. We have three days before you go. During that time, Carson, Tucker, Lord, and Rex have agreed to do two short patrols with the dog to see how he gets along. If by then there are any concerns, we'll leave him behind. If not, he's going with you. Besides, I don't understand why you're so against this; you're the one who rescued him in the first place."

Rogan massaged his eyes with the tips of his fingers. "This is different. It's a big risk, Frank."

"I know," he sighed. "Look, I'm only doing this because I truly believe the dog can help you. I honestly do. You and your men are the best this base has, and I'm scared to hell of losing more of you on this mission. Lord is brilliant at point. Probably the best I've ever seen, but this dog can sense things. I don't know if he smells them or has fucking ESP, but he is a wonder. I wouldn't be ordering this if I thought it wouldn't help."

"Frank, you know you have the respect of every man on this base, myself included. Half these guys would run through a goddamn minefield if you ordered it. So I'll take the dog with us on two conditions: One, I want you to know that I think it's a mistake; and two, if he does anything to threaten our mission, I will kill him."

"Of course," Frank agreed. "Just get in and out as quick as you can, and I promise I'll organize some time off for your platoon."

Frank held out his hand and Rogan accepted it. "How long?"

"Until what?"

"Until we pull out."

"Could be as soon as a month or two. At least that's what I'm hearing."

A sardonic grin danced across Rogan's face. "More than enough time to die, then."

Twenty-nine

Let me get this straight," Wayville said, folding his arms. "We're going to tip and fucking toe our way up the Chi San trail right up into Charlie's heart and pick off two of his top commanding officers, all without any backup?"

"So you were listening," Rogan replied evenly.

"And then we quietly sneak out without Charlie seeing us and skip merrily back down the goddamn yellow brick road?"

"How far back will the drop be?" Gunther frowned.

"Thirty . . . maybe thirty-five clicks."

"*What?* On the Chi San trail, that's a full two-day hike!"

"More like three," Mitchell corrected him.

"Jesus Christ, lieutenant, we've done some crazy shit before, but this is lunacy."

"There's something else: Our intelligence tells us this base holds around three hundred Charlie. And—" He paused, then made a point of looking at each of his men before completing his sentence. "—it's underground."

"A tunnel complex? Fucking great. Why don't we just kill ourselves right now?"

Rogan stepped forward and stared at Wayville. "Calm down and let me finish. I don't like this any more than you do. The bottom line is that we've been ordered to go. We have no choice. Now, we can either sit around and whine about it or we can start planning this thing down to the last fucking detail so that we do everything we possibly can to minimize our risk."

"This is bullshit," Kingston said under his breath.

"For most of you, the biggest risk will be making it to the complex."

"How do you figure that? Once underground, we'll be hunted like rats in a goddamn maze," Gunther insisted.

"Because you're not going in. Only Carson, Lord, and myself are. Carson's going in as our assassin, with Lord and myself as his shadow. Our informant has managed to produce a rough sketch of the complex and has shown us where our two targets will be sleeping. We'll infiltrate at 0300 and be out within an hour. Carson and Lord were approached with the plan yesterday and volunteered to do this."

Kingston was the first to comment. "Chief, you know I normally keep out of these sorts of things, but I can't stay quiet on this one. This can only end badly for us—you know that."

"Not if we plan it properly. If we do our homework and maintain our concentration, chances are we will get through this."

Kingston, like the rest of the platoon, remained unconvinced.

"One last thing. Most of you are aware that we've been testing the dog to see how he behaves out in the field. Our commander feels that we might need his tracking abilities. I've been told the dog has done very well, but be that as it may, I will consider taking him with us only if every man is in agreement. If one of you feels that the dog might in any way compromise us, speak now."

The soldiers exchanged glances with one another, but said nothing.

"All right, then. Fletcher will be his handler, and they'll hike at point with Lord. Gentlemen, we leave in forty-eight hours. As of now, there is no more drinking. Not today and definitely not tomorrow. We're going to be right under Charlie's nose, and trust me, he'll be able to smell the booze on you a mile away."

Thirty

A*nother week, another tense flight over Vietnam,* Fletcher thought as they hovered above the Strip. He knew that if he ever did make it back to the outside world, he would never again set foot in another helicopter.

Holding Jack's leash, he looked down at the Labrador, who was sitting quietly between his legs. He appeared relaxed and at home on board the Huey.

"Where did you come from?" Fletcher whispered in his ear.

Despite the loud drone of the rotors, Jack picked up on the inflection in Fletcher's voice. He swallowed excitedly, turned, and licked him on the cheek.

"You know Jack doesn't belong here. He should be in a painting above a fireplace somewhere. He's too good for this shithole," Travis said, witnessing their exchange.

"That may be, but he sure as hell smells like he belongs here."

Travis smirked, but meant what he said. "There's something about him, Fletcher. He's different. I don't know how or why, but he just is."

"I know. I feel it, too."

"Do you think he's going to cope over the next few days?"

"I do. I mean, you've seen it, Trav—he can smell traps from fifty yards away. He can do it."

The helicopter swooped steeply over a column of tall trees, clearing the top branches by only a few feet. The jungle—a rich palette of earthy tones—stretched between the horizons. It seemed absurd that a war was being waged on such a breathtaking landscape.

"All right, men," Rogan called out, competing with the chopper's engines. "Ten minutes to put down. Time to get real. Get your minds on the game."

The game, Fletcher thought. He had seen men hacked to death, their limbs blown off, and even burnt alive. He had witnessed all manner of depravity, but the description somehow still seemed appropriate. It was a game; only defeat in this context carried a higher price. Just playing it could cost you your sanity.

"I have a real bad feeling about this run," Travis remarked, looking at Fletcher.

"What's to feel bad about? A little hike through the woods, and we'll be on our way home in no time."

"You've chosen a strange time to get positive. Jack must be changing the way you see shit."

"Anything's possible, I suppose."

"Well, this *is* something."

"I just hope Jack brings us some luck," Gunther chipped in. "We could do with one or two of his nine lives."

"A cat has nine lives, you dumb fuck," Wayville said, clicking his tongue. "Jesus, it's a wonder you can tie your own shoelaces."

"You know, for some time now, I've been seriously contemplating sticking my boot—laced or otherwise—up your ass. But I can't figure out which end it is."

The group all laughed; even Wayville smirked at the comeback.

"All right," Rogan said, raising an arm. "Enough with the jokes. It's time to go to work."

Thirty-one

Over the next three days, the Fat Lady's pace was painstakingly slow, as they were forced to hide from numerous NVA patrols in the area. Their movement was further hampered by the constant threat of traps along the trail. Mitchell had so far uncovered more than a dozen that were designed primarily to maim. Jack had already repaid the faith that had been shown in him by sniffing out almost half as many traps, particularly those that involved explosives or still carried human scent.

As nightfall approached, after yet another late afternoon deluge, they were still almost two kilometers away from the tunnel complex. "Lord, Carson . . . we need to get a move on. There's not much light left," Rogan said, marching up behind them.

The rims of Mitchell's eyes were red and swollen from the demands of a long day. "We're moving as fast as we can. I can't afford to go any quicker. The closer we get to the place, the more traps we're likely to come across."

"I understand that, but if we don't make it to the complex in the next twenty minutes, we lose another day. We definitely can't afford that."

"We'll try to shift it up a notch," Fletcher offered.

"You do that."

Mitchell shook his head. "It's pretty fucking risky."

For fifteen minutes, the platoon increased its pace marginally, but the light was rapidly dwindling over the horizon. Already, telltale streaks of pink and purple stretched across the sky.

Again Rogan pulled up behind them. "Time is not our friend. We need to move faster."

"Lieutenant we can't g—"

"Fall back. I'll take over point."

"With respect, Rogan—" Mitchell began.

"This isn't a request, Lord! I'm not asking you to fucking dance. Now fall back. Both of you." With that, he pushed past them and began to run.

"Lieutenant!"

"He's going to get himself killed!" Fletcher cried.

Together they chased after him. They hadn't covered more than fifty yards when Jack suddenly sprinted ahead of them. His sudden burst of acceleration caught Fletcher by surprise, and the leash slipped out of his hand. "Wait, Jack!"

But the Labrador had made up his mind. When he was close enough, he leapt up and bit Rogan on the arm. It was enough to throw him off balance and send him crashing to the ground.

"Release, Jack! *Release!*" Fletcher shouted.

Rogan shoved Jack away and reached for his gun.

Jack, growling now, stood over the lieutenant. He looked ready to attack if Rogan made a sudden move.

"Retreat!" Fletcher commanded as he and Mitchell drew up alongside them.

Rogan's eyes were reduced to thin slits as he stared at the dog. His right arm, muddied and bleeding above the elbow, was fully extended, and his gun was only inches away from Jack's face.

Fletcher moved up alongside the Labrador and gently grabbed him by his collar. "Easy, boy . . . easy."

Rogan looked at Fletcher, as if disoriented, then began to sit up. Jack suddenly leapt at him. This time he snapped at Rogan's face, drawing blood on his cheek.

"Pull your fucking dog back! Now!"

Fletcher battled to restrain Jack. His claws fought for purchase in the mud. Rogan again started to get up, when Mitchell noticed something. "Don't move. Stop!"

Stretched across Rogan's head was a thin trip wire.

"Slide back slowly and keep your head down."

Rogan did as instructed. Mitchell carefully took hold of the trip wire and gently returned it to its position.

Jack immediately relented, the fight gone out of him, and sat down at Fletcher's side, panting happily. By now, the rest of the platoon had caught up to them and had witnessed the incident. The wire was linked to a cluster of hand grenades fixed to the base of a small tree less than ten yards away from them. Another length of wire connected a further eight trees down the path, each with their own cargo of explosives. Had the wire been crossed, it was designed to take out a hundred yards of jungle. It was a platoon killer.

In his first assignment with the Fat Lady, Jack had saved them all.

Thirty-two

Ignoring what had just happened, Rogan returned to point and continued to push forward. Although this time, he moved at a more sensible pace and was accompanied by both Mitchell and Fletcher. What little light remained was rapidly disappearing over the trees. Within minutes, a cloying darkness would descend over them. The night's thumbnail moon would do little to help their cause.

Based on their information, the tunnel complex was now just over a kilometer away. They would soon have to find somewhere to hide until it was time to go in. Once their orders had been executed—all too literally—they would immediately begin their hike back down the path toward the pickup point. Despite the darkness, they would be able to move relatively quickly, as they had disengaged most of the traps on the trail and plotted out the remaining ones on a map. However, plotting the traps was hardly an exact science, and much of the responsibility would again rest on Mitchell and Jack to negotiate a safe passage for them.

As they rounded a bank of trees, Rogan pointed to a slight declivity away from the path that would safely conceal their position. One by one, they filed down the embankment and settled under the dense foliage.

Rogan, Mitchell, and Fletcher sat down together to go over the plan.

"Pearson, we need to review the sketch of the complex. Get over here," Rogan instructed.

Gunther crawled over to them and shone his torch down onto the creased paper. "If our intelligence is accurate, the entrance to the complex is some three or four hundred yards ahead. It's marked by a short wooden stake located between two trees. A trapdoor takes you down about twenty feet to a small crawl space that feeds the main corridor. This corridor runs some five hundred yards south. Off here, you'll find supply rooms, a kitchen, a hospital room of sorts, and the soldiers' barracks. The officers' dormitory lies behind the barracks."

"Okay," Rogan began, removing his pack, "we know that the best time to infiltrate is around 0300. We aren't expecting any heat around the entrance, and if we're lucky, we should be able to get into the main corridor without being detected. The problem comes after that. We don't know how many soldiers are in that room or how difficult it is going to be to access the officers' dormitory."

"We also can't rely on the fact that they'll all be sleeping like angels. Fletch, you're going to have to be pretty sure that none of the soldiers are awake before you go in," Mitchell added.

"And if some of them are?"

"You'll have to wait it out. We've built in a bit of extra time for this, but not much. You've basically got an hour to get in and out. If we exit cleanly by 0400, that gives us probably an hour head start. We can't risk anything less than that," Rogan insisted.

"Where will you two be?"

"Making sure no one comes up behind you, but we won't be shadowing you as close as we'd like. It's too confined in there."

Fletcher knew he was asking the obvious, but proceeded anyway. "What happens if someone raises the alarm?"

Rogan rested his arms on two hand grenades that were secured to the front of his jacket. "We'll take out as many as we can. Make sure the survivors sleep with one eye open for the rest of their goddamn lives."

Fletcher was about to reply, when Jack's ears pricked up.

"Kill the torch," Rogan ordered.

"What is it—?" Gunther began, but was quickly hushed.

For a while, there was nothing. Then slowly they heard it.

Faint voices, like the scent of a dead body in the breeze, wafted toward them.

Thirty-three

The Fat Lady immediately assumed a defensive ring, fanning out as a shadow of the skeletal moon above them. In the purple glow between day and night, the soldiers dropped onto their stomachs, their rifles poised ahead of them.

The voices were coming from the trail, not far away.

In the fading light, Fletcher could see the unease on Rogan's face. It was a concern that extended beyond the voices. The strain of what had happened earlier in the day was clearly still weighing on him. It twisted and churned beneath his skin.

Then, inexplicably, the sound of the approaching men shifted. They no longer appeared to be coming from the trail, but rather from the dense vegetation to their left. They quickly moved around, a blustery wind adding to the deception. They had just adjusted into their new positions when the voices shifted again, except now, impossibly, they seemed to be coming from the earth itself.

Rogan snatched Gunther's torch away from him and shone it onto the ground. The pale yellow orb drifted over a wide square opening covered with a bamboo grid.

It was one of the tunnel's air vents. The voices belonged to the soldiers below.

Rogan quickly signaled for the men to move away from the vent. They quietly slipped farther down the slope, a safe distance away.

"Well, I'll be damned," Gunther murmured.

"Why don't we just drop a few friendly grenades down the vent?" Kingston suggested.

"No good. According to the sketch, the vents are built in an exaggerated *S* structure. The grenades will get caught in the first loop, and all they'll do is collapse the top portion of the vent," Gunther explained. "They won't get anywhere near the men."

"Let's remember why we're here," Rogan interjected. "This is surgical. We're not straying from our orders. In a few hours, we'll take out our marks, and hopefully that'll be the end of it. We'll go in quietly and come out clean. We should be miles down the track before they even discover the bodies."

"Then back home . . . and thank God for that," Wayville added, cupping his hands together in a mock prayer.

"Don't get too ahead of yourself, Rex," Rogan said. "Lord is going to take you through his notes and markings. It's just a contingency, but if he doesn't make it out, it's your responsibility to get the men safely back down the trail."

Wayville's expression soured. "How many traps are we talking?"

"Thirty-seven," Mitchell replied.

"*Thirty-seven?* You sure? Not thirty-eight or thirty-nine?"

"Pretty much."

"Any advice?"

"Yeah, don't step on any wires."

"Funny. Six months we're out in the field together, and now you tell your first joke? Just make sure you do what you have to and get the hell out of there."

"Don't worry, if worse comes to worst, you'll still have Jack here to guide you home."

Jack looked up at Mitchell and all but smiled at the mention of his name.

And in a wink, twilight was gone.

Thirty-four

Fletcher's cheek brushed up against the side of the tunnel. It felt warm and moist against his skin. Apart from the stench of natural decay, he was able to discern a number of other pungent smells, such as stale tobacco, cordite, urine, and even sweat—although most of the latter was probably his own, he thought. Despite the reported size of the complex, the crawl space linking the various areas was minuscule; he had to tuck his elbows in tight against his chest just to squeeze through the opening that joined the entrance section to the main tunnel corridor. He had expected to encounter some form of resistance by now, but so far, the chamber was empty. This wasn't a case of someone shirking his duty, he knew; it was an indictment of how the U.S. was losing the war. Charlie was simply convinced that U.S. troops would not venture this far up the Chi San trail. It was a sign of his growing confidence, his increasing bravado. It was an assumption at least two of his men would pay for with their lives.

Lying at the entrance to the main corridor, Fletcher remained still for a moment, listening for movement. All was quiet. The corridor itself was twice as wide as the entranceway and would allow an average Vietnamese soldier to walk upright. He, however, had to crane his neck and walk with a stoop. He quietly got to his feet and headed toward the faint glow of a lantern some forty yards away. According to their information, the fourth tunnel off to the right of the corridor was the main soldiers' barracks. Behind this area was the officers' dormitory.

He quickly moved toward the pale light and was amazed by how clean and well constructed the complex was. Thick wooden struts supported the roof every few yards. He felt as though he were wandering around a mine. As he neared the lantern, he realized it was hanging on the wall outside the first room. Again, true to their information, it was a supply room. Farther down the corridor was the kitchen. Then a makeshift though empty hospital ward. Until finally, almost two hundred yards farther on, the soldiers' barracks.

Standing alongside, just out of view of the open entranceway, he waited to hear if anyone was talking. Another lantern was positioned on the wall opposite the room, and it cast a soft yellow glow over the sleeping soldiers. There were at least thirty souls lying on the floor, side by side. Strangely, not a single one of them was snoring, or even stirring. They hardly appeared to be breathing.

There's no room to walk, Fletcher suddenly realized.

It had never occurred to him that the men would be lying so close together.

Staring at the sea of bodies, he weighed his options. He could see a door at the back of the room, which he assumed led to the officers' sleeping quarters.

It was some twenty-five yards away, maybe farther. He debated trying to step between the men, but knew there was a strong likelihood that he would get stranded at some point with his path blocked. Or even worse, he might lose his balance and step on one of the men. It was too much of a risk. There remained only one other option.

As part of the support structure of the roof, a single steel beam with a narrow inner railing, much like a railway track, ran the length of the room, ending a yard or so to the right of the back door. Straining his eyes, he studied the steel beam's structure to ensure that there was enough space for him to grip the bar adequately. Although not particularly confident of his assessment, it seemed sufficient. He would climb over the men.

He glanced down at his watch: 0323. He'd been in the complex for more than a quarter of an hour already. Time was running out. He took a deep breath, checked that his gun was properly secured, and grabbed hold of the railing. Without giving it any further thought, he hoisted himself up and began to swing forward. It reminded him of how Kelly used to hang from the monkey bars at her school. He quickly banished the image. Part of him recognized, at least on some level, that what he was doing was either incredibly brave or extraordinarily stupid. The latter seemed more likely.

He had made it almost halfway across the room when the first beads of sweat began to rise up on his forehead. The complex was oppressively hot. A few moments later, he could feel the perspiration dripping off his face. His fingers and hands were showing signs of strain. His shoulders were beginning to tremble.

Below, a soldier stirred and then sat up.

Thirty-five

Fletcher gritted his teeth and lifted his knees to his chest. His fingers were burning with exertion and beginning to slide on the sweat-slicked steel. The soldier looked around the room, muttered something in Vietnamese, and lay back down. A few moments later, he rolled onto his side and was back asleep.

Fighting away the cramp and pain, Fletcher continued forward. Every new reach sapped away his strength. His legs felt like concrete pillars. As he closed in on the back of the room, he was convinced he was going to drop down.

Five yards.

Four.

Three.

Suddenly he lost his grip. Instinctively, he opened his stance and landed with both feet on either side of a soldier's head. He immediately pulled out his gun and pointed it at the man's face. Miraculously, the man remained asleep. Fletcher quickly spun around to check that none of the other men had woken up.

They hadn't.

He couldn't believe his good fortune.

Two inches to either side, and the alarm would've been raised.

He straightened up and carefully stepped over the remaining soldiers. He waited a moment to catch his breath before quietly opening the crudely fashioned bamboo door guarding the entrance to the officers' dormitory. As he moved inside, it felt like he was wading through a pot of black ink. He withdrew his torch, pulled his shirt over the lens to diffuse the light, and switched it on. The room lit up dimly in a sickly green glow. To his surprise, the chamber was almost as big as the soldiers' barracks he had just come through, but housed only the two commanding officers. His marks. This was good news. Even more surprising was that they were both sleeping in a type of bunk bed arrangement at the back of the room.

Perfect, he thought.

Throughout all the planning, his main concern was that, despite the silencer, the sound of the first shot might awaken the second officer before he could get to him. This was now less of an issue.

As he approached the beds, he was gripped by a terrible image.

The cots were so small, it was as though he were preparing to murder a pair of children. In the far reaches of his mind, he felt a smothering, almost overwhelming sadness pass over him. In a matter of months, he'd gone from pushing his daughter on a swing and teaching her to ride her bike to now standing over the bodies of two strangers he was about to murder. Did they have children? Did they deserve to be gunned down in their sleep? Fletcher's precarious world was again threatening to spiral out of control. More often than not, his universe seemed like a basketball spinning on a finger. Just one bump, and the balance would be lost.

He cocked the gun and knelt down next to the man sleeping on the lower bunk. He wrapped a small towel around the barrel to further muffle the sound. His last thought was to wonder what the man was dreaming.

He hoped it was a good dream.

Thirty-six

Closing his eyes, partly out of respect for a dying man and partly for more practical reasons, Fletcher felt his arm recoil and warm blood splatter up his hand and onto the side of his face. The shot sounded like a heavy book dropping off a table—far too loud for the confined space. The second officer shifted around in the bunk above him. The sound of his voice thrust Fletcher into action. He dived on top of his first mark, pressed his gun into the mattress above him, and fired twice.

Blood seeped through the holes.

Taking short, sharp breaths, Fletcher could feel his pulse gallop in the side of his neck.

He was now a murderer, whether it was a war or not. He had only ever killed before in open combat. What he had just done sickened him. For a while, he battled to contain a thick, viscous nausea that churned in his stomach. After what felt like a long time, he eventually managed to lower his gun. His arm was shaking violently. Wiping the syrupy blood off his hand, he reached for his flashlight and checked his watch. He was out of time. He had to get moving now. He sat up and climbed off the dead man.

See the basketball spin, he thought.

With his entire body trembling, he hurried out of the room and slipped back into the soldiers' barracks. Still the men slept peacefully. He looked up at the railing on the ceiling and gathered himself. He placed his fingers into the thin steel groove and hoisted himself up. Surprisingly, his body felt light, and his arms and hands strong—most likely on account of the adrenaline coursing through his veins. He wasted no time and quickly began to swing back across the room.

He was approaching the end of the railing when he noticed something strange ahead of him. In what had been a continuous expanse of bodies covering almost every inch of the floor, there was now an open space about three or four yards from the front of the room.

And then it hit him.

A body was missing.

Fear prickled up the back of his neck. One of the soldiers had woken up and had probably gone to relieve himself. He'd be returning any minute. Fletcher needed to get out of the room and down the passage before the man returned.

His mind urged him forward: *Move . . . move . . . move.*

He reached the end of the railing and dropped down as gracefully as he could.

Still no one stirred, except for the man standing in the doorway.

Thirty-seven

The soldier blinked, his eyes wide with fright, and took a step back.

He was just beyond Fletcher's reach. For a moment, they stared at each other, too startled to react. Fletcher lowered his right hand onto his gun and cupped his left hand over his mouth as a warning to the man to remain quiet. It didn't work. The soldier took a breath and was about to raise the alarm, when a flurry of movement changed everything. Rogan stepped into view and punched the soldier on the side of his head. He was unconscious even before he collapsed into Mitchell's arms. Together, without uttering a word, they shuffled away from the doorway.

Fletcher exhaled, feeling like a man who had narrowly avoided falling off a cliff. *"Jesus fucking Christ!"*

"No . . .'tis the Lord," Mitchell whispered, "and his lieutenant."

"Job done?" Rogan asked calmly, as if the moments preceding his question had not just occurred.

"The marks are down," Fletcher managed, numb, as if the words were not his.

Mitchell carried the soldier back into the barracks and returned him to where he had been sleeping. If another of the soldiers woke up to answer nature's call, it was crucial that everything appeared normal. The Fat Lady needed as much of a head start down the trail as it could get.

As they started back down the main corridor, Fletcher felt a fresh wave of nausea pass over him. This time it would not be denied. More as a reflex than a conscious decision, he doubled over and started to heave. Just as the contents of his stomach began their unnatural journey back up his throat, Mitchell swung his arms around Fletcher's head and forced his hands over his mouth. Rogan quickly added his hands as a further seal.

"Swallow," he said.

Fletcher, with a mouth full of sick, shook his head.

"The sound of your retching will wake up the soldiers, and we will all die," Rogan explained calmly. "You have no choice. Just chew it down. It's all yours, anyway."

Fletcher tried to comply, but as he did, more vomit spewed up his throat.

A thin, watery bile spilled between their fingers.

"Just get it down, and we can get the fuck out of here."

Fletcher cleared his mind and tried to separate himself from his circumstances. It was something he had learned to do effectively in the hospital. After a few seconds, he closed his eyes and managed to swallow the vomit. It felt like thick, warm vegetable soup as it made the return trip down his gullet.

"That's it," Mitchell said, nodding encouragement.

Tentatively, both men removed their hands.

"You okay?" Mitchell asked.

"No."

"Good."

"Is it going to stay down?" Rogan pressed.

"For the moment," Fletcher groaned, wiping away a long string of saliva that was dangling from his chin.

"All right, then, let's move."

They continued down the main corridor and, within minutes, were out of the complex. Pushing through the top of the trapdoor, Fletcher filled his nostrils with the sweet scent of the jungle night. He stumbled out, made half a dozen feet, then dropped to his knees and vomited like a man in the throes of an exorcism.

Although his stomach contents were effectively expelled, the demons remained.

Thirty-eight

The darkness made it difficult for the Fat Lady to progress with any real speed down the trail. Although Mitchell had mapped out the remaining traps ahead of them, the terrain itself prohibited anything more than a brisk walk. Whenever they tried to accelerate, someone would inevitably lose their footing. There was a real danger of one of them getting hurt and hindering their pace even further.

After a while, Travis pulled up alongside Fletcher. "I'm not sure if this is the time, but how'd it go?"

Fletcher shrugged. "For me," he began, still fighting a lingering queasiness, "okay. For the two officers I murdered . . . not so good."

"It couldn't have been easy."

Fletcher stumbled on a loose rock, but reached out for Jack to steady himself. "Taking a life in open combat is one thing. In a firefight, both sides know what's happening, and as shitty as it is, you've each got as much chance of surviving as you do of dying. This was just plain, cowardly murder." He paused. "They looked like goddamn kids in their bunks."

"It's not murder, Fletcher. It's war. You're just following orders."

"War doesn't absolve us of everything. We have to account for some of our actions. Just think of those bastards who ran the death camps in the Second World War. Part of it was duty, but another part was something else. Something a good deal darker. They have to answer for what they did at some point."

"You can't compare what you've just done to what happened at those death camps. It's not the same thing."

"Isn't it?"

"C'mon, Fletch, you know it isn't."

"All I know is this," he uttered, raising his arms up to the pale moonlight. The backs of his hands and the cuffs of his sleeves were smeared black with blood. "This is what's real to me right now."

"We've all got blood on our hands."

"I don't recognize myself anymore. A year ago, I was a different person. Never even thought of owning a gun, let alone firing one. Now I kill people in their sleep."

"I know how you feel. This place has changed things for all of us. I always imagined that at this stage of my life, I'd be happily married, running a small business of some kind. Nothing grand, just something big enough to keep the wolves away from the door. But things seldom turn out the way we want them to. I suppose both our lives have been derailed."

"Thirty-nine," Fletcher said.

"Thirty-nine what?"

"People I've killed since arriving here."

Travis unbuttoned his shirt and was about to respond, when the darkness was lit up by an explosion of angry gunfire.

"*Down* . . . down!" Rogan shouted, preaching to the converted.

Bright bursts of light, the distinctive flares of machine gun fire, crackled to their right from behind a small rise.

Mitchell and Rogan were first to react, immediately returning fire.

How the hell had they wandered into an ambush? Fletcher thought as he fumbled for his rifle, waiting for a bullet to tear through his spine.

The sound of their exchange was thunderous in the dead of morning.

By the time Fletcher had emptied his second clip, he realized they were no longer being fired upon.

"Halt," Rogan instructed. "Hold your fire."

The jungle was quiet, save for the birds that had been disturbed from their nests.

Miraculously, nobody had been shot.

Mitchell and Kingston quickly swept through the area. Once again, and to no one's surprise, Charlie was gone.

All that remained in his wake were the ghosts of bullets—two small mounds of empty shells.

Thirty-nine

After struggling through the stifling midday heat, the Fat Lady finally stopped to rest for a few minutes. Fletcher removed his rucksack and was about to sit down, when he noticed something was amiss with young Craig Fallow. He was kneeling down, holding his head in his hands. Despite his own dubious emotional state and against his better judgment, Fletcher decided to investigate.

"Everything all right, Craig?"

The young man looked up at him, his eyes glistening. He was holding a crumpled photograph of a young woman Fletcher might've found attractive had she not been so heavy.

"Girlfriend?"

"Fiancée," he replied shakily.

"She's pretty. What's her name?"

"Sarah . . . Sarah Evans. Jesus, I miss her." He lifted a hand to his face, more to mask his emotions than to wipe away his tears.

"I'm sorry, it's just . . . *this place* . . . it's a living nightmare. You know?"

Fletcher knew, only too well. In his few months on tour, he'd seen more horror than anything his imagination could ever have conjured up. Innocent villagers executed. Men gutted, strung up in trees. Children torn apart by mines. He'd witnessed a soldier stab himself in the leg to try to get out of combat, succeeding only in severing an artery and bleeding to death. Television footage beamed around the world showed images of spectacular bombings, large artillery fire, and dead bodies being loaded onto choppers, but it failed to capture the real horror of what was happening deep within the bowels of the jungle. The cameras stood and watched from the sidelines while the soldiers were left to inhale the sour stench of the war's breath. But still, the worst part about Vietnam was the waiting. Waiting to trigger a trap. Waiting to walk into an ambush. You could hike through twenty kilometers of thick jungle, singing at the top of your lungs, and emerge unscathed, but the moment you believed you were safe and let down your guard, you were liable to be shot.

Craig rubbed his wrists as if he'd just been released from handcuffs. "I thought I was dead."

"Last night?"

He nodded and removed his helmet. There was a circular dent and scorch mark on its side. "An inch lower, and I'd be gone. Just like that." He traced his fingers over the bullet mark. "It's too much for me."

Fletcher felt for the young man. He was clearly terrified and had every right to be. He was only eighteen and, aside from Fletcher and Travis, the only other soldier in the platoon who had volunteered to serve.

"Why are you here, Craig?"

"You wouldn't believe me if I told you."

"Try me." Fletcher sensed that the youngster wanted to tell him his story.

"To prove a point."

"To whom?"

"Anyone who's ever known me. My parents. My brother. Kids I went to school with. But most of all, to Sarah."

"What are you trying to prove?"

A pause. "My nickname at school was Mr. Gray."

"Doesn't sound that bad. I've heard worse."

"They called me Mr. Gray because I was the guy who no one would remember after school. In their eyes, I was nothing. A nobody. They used to tease me for being a coward and not having a backbone. I got pushed around for so long, it eventually began to feel normal. I guess it's like those women who let their husbands beat them. After a while, they get so used to it that the idea of suddenly doing something about it seems absurd. Maybe even impossible."

"So you came out into this madness?"

Craig looked back down at the photograph. "I wanted Sarah to be proud of me. To know that she was marrying a real man, not someone who wouldn't be able to look after her. You have to understand, she was at school with me. She saw what the other kids would say and how I always backed down. I couldn't go on having her think I was weak. Hell, I also needed to prove it to myself. There's nothing worse in life than feeling helpless." More tears welled up in his eyes. "The irony is that it's all true. I *am* a fucking coward! This place is killing me."

"Hey, that's bullshit! Just by pitching up here, you've shown more courage than any of your classmates. And you're right to be scared. Only a lunatic would be enjoying himself down here. We're all scared shitless, I promise you. Last night I was so goddamn afraid, I puked my guts out."

Fletcher's words did little to console Craig Fallow. The teenager was on the verge of a breakdown, and nothing but a flight out of Vietnam was going to help him. Even that, Fletcher knew, could be too late.

As he watched the youngster lovingly fold the photo of his fiancée and return it to his pocket, he realized something that he knew was true the moment it entered his mind: Craig Fallow was in a world of trouble, whatever his future held.

Forty

It was late afternoon the following day when they finally reached the extraction point. The men were all dead on their feet; few even had the energy left to make casual conversation. The relief of surviving their assignment was eclipsed by their exhaustion. Jack, in particular, looked stiff and sore from their journey. It was the farthest he had traveled, by some margin, since his recovery.

Fletcher looked across to Craig Fallow, who was once again poring over his fiancée's photo. His desperation to get home to her was plain to see. Fletcher was trying to recall what the young Sarah Evans looked like, when a distant crack, almost like the sound of a tree being felled, echoed behind them. If it was gunfire, it was a distance away.

"Lord, Rex . . . check it out," Rogan instructed in a hushed voice, passing Mitchell his binoculars. The two men stood up and hurried over to a short but steep hill behind them.

As Fletcher watched them climb the embankment, a second crack issued out from the same area, slightly louder this time.

"Stay down," Rogan ordered.

As Fletcher watched Mitchell reach the top of the rise, something made him look back. "Oh, Christ."

Sitting with his legs folded, Craig Fallow had his head bowed down over his lap. The front of his shirt was stained bright red.

"Edgar, get to Craig now!"

As they scrambled to his side, blood was already gushing from his throat. Edgar shoved a bandage into the wound to try to stem the flow, but it was immediately saturated.

"Craig! Wake up, son. . . . *wake up!*" Kingston said, squeezing his hand.

Edgar tore away the front of his shirt to try to get a better look at the boy's wound. Sheets of blood flowed down his chest. He listened for a heartbeat and, discovering none, immediately began to administer CPR.

But it was no good.

After almost ten minutes of compressions, Rogan pulled him away. "Stop it, son. He's gone. There's nothing more you can do for him. Leave him be."

Edgar, a teenager himself, had to bite back the tears; his hands and face were covered in his friend's blood. "What just happened here?" he asked in little more than a whisper.

Rogan helped the young medic to his feet. "Vietnam," he sighed. "Fucking Vietnam."

The bullet that had robbed Craig Fallow of the opportunity of a happy life with the woman of his dreams had done so purely by chance. It was discharged from too far away to be an intentional strike.

Mercifully, he never felt what hit him. His life was lost before he knew it was in jeopardy. The bullet entered through the top of his forehead and exited through his neck, suggesting it had been fired randomly into the air. Had he been wearing his helmet, his life might well have been spared.

Fletcher leaned over the young man's lifeless body and covered his face with his bandanna. He wondered grimly if fate had been stalking the troubled soldier. It had missed its mark the previous night; had it conspired to return for him today?

After all, Fletcher had felt fate's shadowed side before.

He reached into Craig's lap and retrieved the crumpled photograph of the one bright light in his life. In time, a soldier or an official from the army would notify his family of his death. The communication would simply state that Infantryman Craig Fallow had died fighting for his country and that the United States was indebted to them for his sacrifice.

But that wasn't good enough.

Right then, Fletcher resolved to write his first letter in Vietnam. In it, he would tell of how well liked and respected Craig was by his platoon. He would describe how he had defended the lives of numerous villagers and once even helped rescue a captured pilot. He would tell young Sarah Evans how much she was loved and how Craig had died with her photograph clutched in his hand. And he would let them know that Craig Fallow was the most courageous young man he had ever known.

And it would all be true, every last word.

Forty-one

Fletcher closed his eyes and tried to tune out the drone of the helicopter's rotors. He could no longer bear the sight of Craig Fallow's bloodied corpse. Instead, he imagined he was sitting on a perfect golden beach, the early morning sun shimmering off the ocean. The image evoked the memory of a holiday he and his girls had shared only two years ago. He remembered Kelly, who had built an elaborate sand castle too close to the shoreline, working furiously to build a moat to protect her handiwork.

"Mommy . . . Daddy . . . help me! Quick, the water's going to wash away my castle!"

Abigail, who was tanning, stood up and rushed to her daughter's side. "C'mon, Fletch, help us defend the kingdom."

Fletcher reluctantly set aside his newspaper and joined his girls. Together, the three of them dug a deep moat around the front and sides of the castle. But no matter how hard they worked, the waves kept coming, each onslaught filling the hastily dug channel. Eventually the incoming tide overwhelmed the castle, melting its sculpted edges and reducing it to a blurred, indistinct mound.

After watching her creation be destroyed, Kelly looked up at her father. She never said anything, but Fletcher saw it in her eyes. She was disappointed in him. She was upset that he wasn't able to save something of hers.

He was her father: He was supposed to protect her.

That innocently conceived but accusing expression had haunted Fletcher since the crash. The sand castle became a natural metaphor for her death. Just as he could not protect her sculpture, so he had failed to save her from that nightmarish December morning. Sometimes, just that single thought threatened to consume him.

A familiar weight pressed against his thigh, rousing him from his daydream. It was Jack. In his first assignment, he had performed far beyond everyone's expectations. Fletcher couldn't help but feel proud of how well he had fared. As he watched the Labrador drift off to sleep, familiar questions swirled around in his mind.

Where had he come from? Was he truly a Vietnam war dog?

He couldn't shake the nagging feeling that Jack was somehow lost, as if he had been headed elsewhere, but then for some reason strayed from his path.

Trying to avoid the depressing sight of Craig's inanimate frame, Fletcher stared out the cabin window. The jungle passed below in a familiar brown and green montage. A herd of water buffalo marched across a wide shallow river. Young boys rode on their backs, seemingly oblivious of the war or the sound of the helicopter above them. Fletcher imagined a comparison between them and boys of their age in America. They may as well have been a species from another planet, such was the gulf between them.

From deep in his thoughts, he felt Jack move away from him. He watched with interest as Rogan fished out two biscuits from his pocket and offered them to Jack. Unsure of the lieutenant, the Labrador edged forward and gently accepted the treats from him. As soon as they left his hand, Rogan turned away and stared out the door as if the moment had never happened.

Forty-two

When they arrived back at base, there was little time to say good-bye to Craig Fallow. He was to be placed in a body bag, cataloged, and hastily scheduled for a series of flights out of Vietnam. Having corpses lying around wasn't particularly good for base morale.

However, before they would allow him to be taken away, the Fat Lady carried his body down to their church. It was little more than a tent featuring a crudely fashioned wooden cross, a spattering of candles, and half a dozen wooden benches, but it sufficed.

This was the way they always bade farewell to one of their own.

Army procedure wasn't about to change that.

Kingston was a deeply religious man and was always tasked with saying a few words and reciting a passage of choice from the Bible—a book he kept clutched firmly under his arm most days when on base. During the prayer, Fletcher glanced up at Rogan and could see the emotion cutting into his face.

When Kingston was done, Fletcher stood up and took a long, slow breath. "Up until recently, I knew very little about Craig Fallow. He was the kind of young man who kept to himself. Which is a pity, because I was fortunate enough to get to know him a little over the past few days, and now I truly understand what we've lost. Craig came here believing that he needed to prove something to himself and to his family, and in the end, it cost him his life. The tragedy is that he didn't need to prove anything. Who Craig Fallow was . . . *was enough.* I will never forget the courage he showed when we were defending that small village that Charlie was terrorizing. I'm sure we all remember how, during the firefight, he ran out from his position, putting himself deep in the line of fire, to protect a mother and her child as they ran for cover."

Fletcher paused and then wiped his eyes. "Our hearts go out to his family and, in particular, to Sarah Evans, his young fiancée. May we keep them all in our thoughts and in our prayers."

"Amen." Kingston nodded.

A few minutes later, they all went their separate ways. Rogan would have to report back on their assignment while the rest of the platoon would either drop by the field hospital for a few running repairs or retire to their bunks to be alone with their thoughts—and, of course, the guilt of being alive.

As Fletcher returned to his tent, he was determined to write Craig Fallow's loved ones an epitaph that would elevate his legacy above the apparent wretchedness of his adolescent life. Maybe then, Mr. Gray would be remembered.

The next two weeks drifted by without incident. As promised, the Fat Lady was rewarded with the entire period off. The majority of the men took the opportunity to pursue the rich palette of carnal pleasures on offer at any number of towns and villages in the southern reaches of Vietnam. Fletcher and Travis, however, remained behind to look after Jack. They spent most of their time training him and developing his skills. If he was to accompany them on more assignments, it was important he learn additional hand and voice commands.

His progress was unreal. Within a few days, they had taught him twenty individual commands. This included an instruction to detach from the Fat Lady and track them down at a later time. The idea was that if they came under heavy fire, it would be safer for Jack to leave the area and return to them later. He had absorbed and learned each command with vigor, always eager to gain their approval.

Jack became as much a feature of life on the Strip as the smell of diesel and cordite. Those who hadn't been dog lovers before the war now enjoyed having Jack around. He brought a sense of family and lightheartedness to the base. Even the commander had become partial to him, ordering a special leather harness for his upcoming patrols.

One morning, a few of the men took it upon themselves to build Jack a special eight-foot-wide steel bath that he could wade around in to cool off. To get him to use it, Fletcher and Travis climbed into the tub and, while trying to coax him into the waist-high water, found it a most agreeable place to see out the afternoon. So they stayed. The next day, they brought beers with them and remained until well after sunset. They spent their hours sitting on either side of Jack, reminiscing over happier times back home. Their conversations ranged from sport and films—a passion they both shared—to travel and food. Their exchanges remained light and whimsical, circling away from the darker areas of their pasts. Jack, like all dogs, was just content to be in the company of his owners.

For a while, life in Vietnam was bearable. The problem, however, remained that one could have twenty-three good hours in a day and then one that left you with a bullet in your spine and a column of air where a limb used to be.

As they approached the end of their R & R, Fletcher and Jack were virtually inseparable. Wherever Fletcher went, Jack followed. Whether it was to the ablutions block, the munitions store, or the Soup, the Labrador was always in tow.

When they finally returned to duty, the Fat Lady was sent on two short assignments, both fairly minor incursions of a day each. Jack accompanied them on each occasion and twice sniffed out traps that might otherwise have proved fatal.

Jack was no longer simply a dog they had found or even the base's mascot.

He was a soldier.

Theirs.

Forty-three

Gunfire ripped through the jungle.

Fletcher grabbed Jack by his harness and scrambled toward a bank of nearby trees. Glancing over his shoulder, he saw Rogan lying on his back, his M16 bucking against his chest as he returned fire. "Cover . . . cover!" he shouted, urging his men to safety.

As Fletcher rounded the trees and reached for his rifle, he realized too late that he was at the top of a steep embankment. There was nothing he could do to prevent himself from falling down the back of it. The mud and slick grass made it impossible for him to halt his slide. He clawed desperately at the ground, his hands and feet slipping in the mire. As the sickening sound of automatic gunfire continued to punctuate the air, he realized that Jack hadn't fallen with him. His heart sank as he imagined the Labrador lying dead at the foot of the trees. In a wild frenzy, he punched and kicked his way back up to the top of the slope, desperate to get back to the dog.

The first thing he saw was a soldier lying on his side about fifty yards down the trail. Jack was standing over him. His hackles were raised, and he was growling and snapping in the direction of the onslaught. Snarling, he exposed his teeth, trying to ward off the attackers. The rest of the Fat Lady had managed to find cover and were returning fire.

All except Rogan.

He was running toward Jack and the downed soldier.

Fletcher immediately joined in the chase. Bullets exploded into the ground around Jack and the soldier, but even when two rounds tore into the man's back, Jack stood firm, refusing to relent. Fletcher's breath caught in his throat when he realized who the soldier was.

"No . . ."

Another volley tore into Travis's legs, and blood splattered up Jack's flank. Suddenly Jack bit into the side of Travis's shirtsleeve and tried to drag him away.

Fletcher's heart lurched at the sight. He held out his rifle in one hand and, without looking, opened fire into the hill. Part of him was aware that he was screaming, desperate to make up the ground. "Fuck you . . . fuck you!" he cried, throwing his gun down as the clip ran out.

A bullet tore through a fold in his pants, grazing his leg.

Another pinged off the back of his helmet.

He was a natural athlete and was right behind Rogan the moment he reached Travis. In one fluid movement, the lieutenant swooped down and grabbed the front of Travis's shirt and lifted him up as if he weighed no more than a few pounds. Fletcher scooped up Jack, and together they scrambled for cover. They had no sooner collapsed to the ground than the firing stopped.

Mitchell called out to them from the hill. He had flanked their attackers and taken them out. "Hold your fire! All Charlie down."

"Edgar!" Rogan screamed. "Get here!"

Fletcher crawled next to Travis and cradled his friend's head in his hands while Edgar checked his wrist for a pulse.

"Christ," Gunther uttered as the men got sight of their friend's injuries. Travis's chest had taken at least five rounds. It was impossible to make out how many hits the lower half of his body had sustained. A thick pool of black blood arced around his legs and waist.

Edgar wiped away some of the blood and began to tear off his clothes.

"Travis . . . can you hear me?" Fletcher asked, rubbing the side of his face.

His eyes stirred, but remained closed.

"C'mon, man . . . *please.*"

Slowly, he opened his eyes. "Fletch . . ."

"Yeah, Trav . . . it's me. It's all over."

The whites of Travis's eyes were outlined in blood. "Did you see Jack?" he asked quietly, his teeth coated red. "Did you see what he did?"

"I saw."

"He tried to save me. Can you believe that?"

Fletcher nodded, unable to reply.

Edgar was trying to stem the blood flow, but it was useless.

Travis choked, then looked up peacefully at the sky. "It's true what they say, you know."

"What is?" Fletcher managed, feeling his friend's blood spread under his knees.

"How calm everything becomes before you die."

Fletcher wanted to tell him he was going to make it, but couldn't bring himself to lie. "Please, Trav . . . don't."

"It's all right, Fletch, it's okay. Especially for guys like you and me."

The comment was lost on most of the men, but Fletcher nodded as fresh tears cut a trail through the grime on his cheeks.

"Look after Jack. He deserves to get out of this place. Take him to Miami. Let him run on the beach."

Fletcher's chin trembled. "I will. You have my word."

"Make sure you have a view of the ocean . . ."

". . . and crisp, fresh sheets." Fletcher smiled but there was no humor in his expression.

"If I see your girls, I'll tell them how much you miss them."

As Travis took his final breath, Fletcher bent over and spoke into his ear. "Go to your wife . . . she's waiting for you."

He squeezed Fletcher's hand, and although his eyes remained open, the vital light that Mitchell had once spoken of was gone.

Forty-four

The weight of Travis's death pressed heavily on each of the men as they flew back to base. His body was wrapped and bound in sleeping bags, but blood still seeped through. Jack was sitting alongside Fletcher with his head perched on his knee, staring at Travis's body. Although Fletcher couldn't be certain, particularly above the sound of the rotors, he was convinced he could hear Jack whining. He leaned forward and gently rubbed the side of his neck. The Labrador's expression projected a deep and primal sadness; he understood the language of death.

"It wasn't our fault, Jack," Mitchell called out, recognizing the look in the dog's eyes. "They were downwind of us almost two hundred yards. There's nothing we could've done. We never had a chance."

Kingston, who had not uttered a single word since the ambush, began to sing "Amazing Grace." He closed his eyes and let his baritone fill the cabin. His faith, which had never wavered despite all the atrocities he had witnessed, gave him an inner strength that Fletcher envied. Sometimes, though, he wondered how Kingston could believe so single-mindedly in a god that allowed the nightmare of Vietnam to persist. His own faith, which at its most resolute had not held much conviction, had been eroded over the past two years. Every death was another wave overwhelming it. He knew that real faith should be able to weather any storm. But his defenses, however frail, were all but overcome.

He knew he was on the verge of a final, decisive breakdown. There were just too many dead faces to contend with. Too much loss. While he thought of this and other nightmares, he allowed Kingston's song into his heart. It was a whisper against the screams of the dead.

Before the helicopter even touched down, it was clear something important had happened on base. As they came in to land, they could see men running, hugging, and punching the air. One soldier was on his knees, holding his head in his hands.

As the Fat Lady disembarked, Fletcher remained behind.

He already knew why they were celebrating. There could be only one explanation for their behavior.

As the pilot cut the engine and the rotors lost their will, Fletcher watched one of the soldiers run up to Wayville and Gunther. He was so excited, he couldn't help himself from leaping into the air, despite the vague threat of decapitation.

Fletcher couldn't hear what he was saying, but the shape of his words was unmistakable.

"It's over! It's over!" he cried. "We're going home!"

Fletcher closed his eyes and shook his head. He felt sick.

In the dying embers of the war, Travis might well have been Vietnam's final casualty.

At least among the dead.

Forty-five

They had all known it was coming, but the wheels of bureaucracy often took so long to turn that an official conclusion to the war could have been years away. Few expected the end to arrive as suddenly as it did.

As they disembarked from the helicopter, they learned that a cease-fire had been signed by the United States, South Vietnam, North Vietnam, and the Vietcong. The agreement stipulated that U.S. and allied forces be withdrawn from Vietnam's borders and that all prisoners—on both sides—be released within sixty days. The pact also permitted North Vietnam to leave 150,000 troops in the south and called for internationally supervised elections to decide the course of the country's political future.

In short, the war was over.

But before they could properly process the news, the Fat Lady had to tend to their own. Just as they had done with Craig Fallow, they carried Travis down to their church to pay their final respects. Entering the tent, they gently placed his body underneath the cross and all lowered down onto one knee. Without needing to refer to his Bible, Kingston recited a few psalms as well as a passage Fletcher recognized from Revelations. After a long prayer, Kingston began to sing "Abide with Me," but for once his emotions got the better of him and he could not complete the hymn. Despite the sounds of revelry outside, each of the men remained behind for a long while, taking their time to say good-bye. Eventually, one by one, they lifted to their feet and drifted out of the tent until only Fletcher and Mitchell were left behind.

"I can't believe he's gone," Fletcher remarked, his voice barely registering.

By his very nature, Mitchell was a man of few words. He spoke sparingly, as if dialogue were vital ammunition that needed to be conserved. Thus, his reply surprised Fletcher. "I know how close you were. You were a very good friend to him." He paused. "And in this place, that really means something."

Fletcher smiled, tears stinging his eyes. "He was a good man. A *good man*. He should never have been here."

Mitchell nodded, but said nothing in return.

"At least," Fletcher offered, his voice wavering, "he's back with his wife now."

Mitchell reached across and placed his hand on Fletcher's shoulder, but did not speak again. He had no more words left in his arsenal.

That night, almost every man, woman, and dog got drunk. Most indulged not only to celebrate surviving the darkness of Vietnam and the prospect of returning home to their families, but also to remember those who had been lost.

As Fletcher nursed his beer, he imagined similar scenes of joyousness at bases throughout Vietnam. Never had a defeat been so welcomed. The real jubilation, of course, was happening north of them. As he looked around the Soup, the soldiers' excitement was plain to see. For so long, the horror of Vietnam had been their lives, and now—within weeks—they would all be back home. He imagined wives running into the arms of their husbands, children into the arms of their fathers. The genuine sense of warmth and happiness he felt for them was tempered by the thought of the thousands of families who would never again be reunited and by the fate that awaited the people of South Vietnam. Fletcher knew the cease-fire would ultimately break down, and without American support, the South would soon be overpowered. The U.S. and allied effort, despite its enormous firepower, had been brought to its knees. Against such determined and resourceful opposition, the South stood no chance on its own.

"To Travis," Gunther said, raising his beer.

"And to every other mother's son who died in this hellhole," Wayville added.

"Hear, hear," the room chorused.

Although Fletcher rarely contributed, the conversation roamed from some of the lighter moments on base to what they were all planning to do when they got home.

The drinking never slowed.

But the more Fletcher drank, the more sober he felt. He'd hoped the alcohol might numb him to the effects of the day, but it seemed only to fuel his depression. After struggling through his third beer, he decided he'd had enough. As he and Jack left the Soup and headed toward their tent, he noticed a man sitting on a rock in the open field. Although it was very dark, there was no mistaking his frame. He had seen it often enough under the cover of night to know who it was. "Getting some air?" he called out.

Rogan turned. "Carson . . . what are you doing out here?"

"The beer tasted off. How about you?"

"As you said. Getting some air."

"Want some company?"

"Sure."

Fletcher and Jack sat down a few yards away from the lieutenant, and for a while, both men were quiet.

"I've been out here for almost an hour. So far, I've counted over five hundred stars. I wonder how long it took to lose our first five hundred men in this place."

"Forget it, lieutenant. It'll drive you mad just thinking about it."

"So many lives lost for a failed cause."

"I understand how you feel—"

"With respect, Fletcher, I'm not sure you do. I really believed in what we've been trying to achieve here. Maybe it's why I've lasted this long," he said, then slowly began to shake his head. "We're sending the South to their deaths. You know that, don't you?"

Fletcher shifted onto his haunches and, instead of answering the question, decided to change gears. "Are you going to stay in the service?"

"I don't know. I can't see myself getting a normal job like selling fucking cars, can you?"

Fletcher smiled at the thought. "Look, for what it's worth, thank you."

"For what?"

"Keeping us alive."

"You've got to be shitting me."

"I'm not. Without you and Mitchell, none of us would've survived."

"That's not true, and you know it. For the most part, we were just lucky. Hell, if it wasn't for Jack, here, we wouldn't be having this conversation."

The Labrador had curled up between the two men and was already fast asleep.

"If he hadn't stopped me before that wire—"

"That's one time. How many other times have you saved us?"

Rogan looked back up into the night. "I wasn't able to save Travis."

"You did everything you could. What you did today was probably the most courageous thing I've ever seen. How you didn't get yourself killed, I'll never know."

"If I recall, you were running behind me."

"That's different."

"How?"

"You were drawing their fire."

"Bullshit. Besides, I'm not the one with the death wish."

"Listen, I—"

"You think I don't know why you came out to Vietnam? I know what happened to you . . . and to your family. But as much as it might burn you, the world hasn't had enough of you yet," Rogan countered. "So what're you going to do with your life now? Try to find another war? Put a gun in your mouth?"

"I couldn't. Who'd look after Jack?"

"Is that what it comes down to?"

Fletcher didn't respond.

"Is the line that thin for you?"

"Isn't it for everyone?"

"You tell me."

"Travis was half an hour away from surviving this place. I'd say that's a thin line."

"I'll give you that, but the difference is, he wanted to live."

Fletcher shrugged, but again did not respond.

Rogan reached across and rubbed the side of Jack's face. "You know . . . this damn animal really grows on you."

"I know."

"I'm glad he made it. He's going to love America."

"I think so, too." Fletcher nodded. "Do you know when we're scheduled to pull out?"

"There'll be a full briefing tomorrow morning, but the men aren't going to like it. Because of our advanced position, we're one of the last bases to leave."

Forty-six

By the time Fletcher reached his tent, he could barely keep his eyes open. The emotion of the day had taken its toll on him. He tried to ignore Travis's empty bunk, but his eyes were drawn to it. Some of Travis's personal effects—photographs and books, mostly—were stacked together on a small bedside table. The sight of them depressed Fletcher even further. He knew he would have to sort through them and have them packaged and sent home, just not tonight. He was about to collapse onto his bed, when he noticed a large brown envelope on his pillow with a short note attached to it. Intrigued, he sat down and removed the note.

Carson,

This came for you a few weeks ago. It was found at the bottom of one of the mailbags this afternoon. Sorry.

Lifting the envelope, he immediately recognized the handwriting on its cover. It was the same scrawl that had often blotted his articles. It was from Marvin Samuels, his old friend and former editor. Judging by the size of the package, he imagined it contained a few back issues of *The Mirror*. As he tore it open and removed its contents, he realized he was only half right. There were three back issues of the paper inside, complete with highlighted articles about Vietnam, but there was also a second, smaller envelope.

For no particular reason, he felt his pulse quicken.

The envelope contained a one-page letter attached to a further document.

Dear Fletcher,

I hope these words find you, and find you well.

You should know that your efforts are greatly appreciated by scores back here, but equally many are against our nation's ongoing presence in Vietnam. It saddens me to tell you that some soldiers returning home are being ostracized and treated like criminals. I would like to inform you otherwise. I would like to tell you that you and your fellow officers can expect ticker tape parades when you get back. I would like to tell you that the American people have appreciated the blood that's been spilled to protect their way of life.

But I would be lying.

I hope it's enough for you to know that cowards like myself are very grateful for what you are doing and are indebted to your sacrifice.

I feel sick about the way things ended between us at the cemetery, and I'm truly sorry for my part. Having said that, I fear I have placed an even greater risk on our friendship by what I am about to reveal.

Attached to this letter are thirty-nine pages of a diary your wife kept.

Your mother found it in a box during the sale of your home and came to me nearly beside herself. She didn't know what to do with it. God knows, neither did I. She felt that if she sent it to you, it might just make what you are going through all that much more difficult to endure. Or it might—please let me be right—raise your spirits.

I've kept these pages in my drawer for months under lock and key. Every day, I've debated sending them to you—and every day, I've found a reason not to.

But they're beginning to burn a hole through my desk, through my heart. Neither your mother nor I have read beyond the first page, its content was never intended for us. In the end, I would rather regret the things that I've done than those I never had the courage to do. Whatever the outcome.

I pray that these pages go some way to mending the hurt that you live with. Selfishly, I hope they bring me to a day when I can again be in the company of my friend and tell him how proud I am of him. And how much I've missed him.

May God keep you until that day.

Your friend,
Marvin

Despite the heat, Fletcher felt his hands go cold. He had no idea Abby kept a diary. With his heart racing, he unfolded the pages. He managed to read the first few words before he was overcome. Abigail had addressed the diary to Kelly, who at the time of writing, had not yet been conceived. It was a mother writing a diary of her life, which she one day intended to give to her daughter.

It began: *Kelly, my angel, today I met the man I know I'm going to marry. Today, I met your father.*

Forty-seven

The weeks that followed were all about packing up supplies and loading them onto helicopters. The sound of choppers taking off and landing became a constant background noise, like great mechanical bees cross-pollinating through an industrial meadow. Late afternoons were spent mainly at leisure, with many of the men whiling away their time playing baseball or touch football. Their games were largely uninterrupted, as the afternoon rains had all but dried up. Even the morbid heat, that for so long had clung to them like a second skin, lifted now. The nights, whatever the weather, were for drinking.

While under the spell of alcohol, the men often became emotional. They shared photographs of loved ones. They got into shallow and meaningless arguments. They told stories of home. They reread old letters. They cried over their children. They planned proposals.

They were all slowly coming to terms with surviving Vietnam and the prospect of life beyond it. Senior officers kept order, but allowed the men more than their fair share of freedom. As the days ebbed closer to their departure, laughter returned to many of them. The dark cloud that had hung over the Strip for so long was finally beginning to lift.

With just under two weeks to go until their withdrawal, Fletcher was on his way to the medical tent to set up one final dip for Jack when a man called out to him.

"Fletcher," the voice said, jogging up behind him. "Wait up. This came for you."

It was Wayne Bradley. He was responsible for the base's mail. He was carrying a crumpled brown envelope.

"Thanks, Wayne."

The soldier flashed him a thumbs-up and jogged off.

With so few days left, Fletcher couldn't imagine whom the letter was from. For a moment, he wondered if Marvin had somehow come across another part of Abby's diary.

He savored every word of the thirty-nine pages he had been sent before. Her entries were all about their courtship, and although they told him very little that he didn't already know about his wife, it afforded him a precious glimpse back into their early life together, a portal through time. The emotion of her writing was difficult to bear, but he welcomed her words much in the same way a man without hope welcomes an oncoming train. But the meager weight of this new letter suggested no further connection to Abby.

He tore open the fold at the top of the envelope. Inside was a single-page letter.

He unfolded it and instantly recognized the name at the bottom of the page.

Dear Fletcher,

Letters are strange things. Although we have never met, the correspondence we have exchanged over the last few months has led me to believe that, at least on some level, we've grown to know each other.

My squad and I have greatly enjoyed helping you get Jack rehabilitated and have taken much pleasure in hearing of his many successes out in the field.

However, as much as I wish this wasn't the case, I am the bearer of extremely bad news.

If you don't already know what I'm referring to, I suggest you sit down and brace yourself.

It appears as though the price of withdrawing troops and equipment from Vietnam is proving too costly for our government.

I'm afraid there is no easy way to say this. Fletcher, our dogs have been officially declared "surplus military equipment" and are not being allowed to return home with us.

We've been ordered to hand them over to the South Vietnamese. Those that aren't are being euthanized or just left to die.

It's a nightmare for all us dog handlers. Some four thousand dogs have been fighting in this war and giving their lives to save American soldiers, and they are now being abandoned by our government.

I'm fighting this with everything I have, but in truth, I don't hold out much hope. I've been in contact with other dog units, and they've been forced to leave their dogs behind, on some occasions at gunpoint. Other handlers have been arrested for showing resistance.

If I somehow manage to organize safe passage for our dogs, I'll send for Jack. But it's not looking good. We're due to leave in a few days. If you haven't received word from me by March 13, then I have failed. In which case, I pray you have better luck.

I'll be thinking of you and Jack.

Your friend,
W. Wallace

Fletcher's mind was reeling. How could the government be doing this? he thought. *How can they just abandon the dogs?* This couldn't be happening. Surely the American public would be up in arms about it.

With trembling hands, he reread his friend's letter.

. . . If I somehow manage to organize safe passage for our dogs, I'll send for Jack. But it's not looking good. We're due to leave in a few days. If you haven't received word from me by March 13, then I have failed. . . .

The letter slipped from Fletcher's grasp and, despite the gravity of its message, floated gracefully to the ground.

It was March 15.

Forty-eight

This is bullshit!" Fletcher shouted. "How can you abide by this?"

"What would you have me do, Fletcher? I've been given orders right from the top."

"So what? This is wrong! Everyone knows it!"

"You think I like this? I know it's cruel. Damn it, man, I was right behind you in getting Jack on his feet again. But—"

"But what? Please tell me. These dogs are soldiers. How can we just leave them behind, for Christ's sake?"

Hearing their raised voices, a soldier opened the door just wide enough to look in.

"It's all right," Frank said. "Leave us."

Fletcher began to pace across the room.

"I know this is hard for you. It's difficult for all of us: Jack is like part of the family."

"Really?" Fletcher announced, his voice thick with sarcasm. "If Jack were your son, would you leave him behind? Would you leave him here to die?"

"That's not fair."

"Neither is this! Look, this is the way I see it: Jack is the only dog on base. It'll be a hell of a lot easier to smuggle him off than it would be if we had a dog unit. In fact, the heartless bastards on Capitol Hill don't even know he exists."

"I'm sorry, but I can't go against senior orders. I'm not jeopardizing a thirty-year career in the military for this. It's ludicrous."

"Nothing will happen to you! You won't be implicated! I'll get him on one of the choppers, and I'll deal with whatever consequences there are. C'mon, Frank, this is just a cost-saving exercise."

The commander closed his eyes and pinched the bridge of his nose with his thumb and index finger. "I've done all that I can. I've contacted everyone I know who might've been able to help us with this. Besides, even if we got Jack off base, what good would it do? There are at least three flights between here and America. There's no way you would get it done."

"He deserves a chance, Frank. Please . . . let me try."

"No, Fletcher, it's over. The government's taking a hard line on this. There's nothing more either of us can do now. Why don't you focus on the positives here? You're going home in a few days. You have the rest of your life to look forward to. Start putting your energies into that."

Fletcher snatched his hat off the table and headed for the door. "How can you be so goddamn weak?"

Frank's expression hardened. "I've had about enough of your attitude. Do I need to remind you who you're talking to?"

"Don't worry. I know *exactly* who I'm talking to.'

"If you think—"

"The really sad thing is that up until today, I had nothing but the utmost respect for you."

"We're not finished, this—"

"Oh, we're finished," Fletcher insisted, pushing through the door, "and for what it's worth . . . *fuck you.*"

Forty-nine

Fletcher spent his final days in Vietnam desperately trying to devise a plan to smuggle Jack back to America. Although there were enough people willing to help him, there were too many controls and logistical hurdles to overcome. He discovered that the trip home actually involved four flights and several transfers, and he simply didn't have the contacts down the line to sustain the effort. There were also too many intangibles, too many things that could go wrong. The obvious temptation was to hide Jack in a crate, but the risk of him freezing to death in the various cargo holds forced Fletcher to abandon the idea. He wrote letters, set up meetings, spoke to other dog units, even called old press contacts back home, but one way or another, each avenue soon reached a dead end. He even tried appealing to senior politicians, but they would not be swayed. Most of them couldn't care less what happened to the dogs. To them, it was hardly an issue. The animals were just equipment—like rifles and tents—now surplus to requirements.

With less than a week left, the days quickly bled out.

Despite all their initial support, even the Fat Lady had abandoned hope. Their conversations now focused almost exclusively on their lives back home and their future plans. Some of them hardly even looked at Jack anymore. To most of them, he was already dead, another ghost from the nightmare of Vietnam. Fletcher felt betrayed by the ease with which they had resigned themselves to Jack's fate. As a result, he stopped talking to them altogether. Instead, he spent his hours alone with Jack, savoring their time together. He kept trying to imagine what it would feel like, having to leave him behind.

He imagined the look of confusion in the Labrador's eyes, the sense of abandonment.

How long would he survive on his own? he wondered.

A few days? A month?

What would claim him in the end? Starvation, heat stroke, disease? Or would his life finally draw to a close on the tip of Charlie's knife? A soldier had suggested that Jack be shot now to save him from the undoubted suffering that lay ahead.

Not since that day out on the hospital balcony back in Chicago had Fletcher felt more alone. With only a day left before their withdrawal, he found a secluded place near the base's perimeter, where he and Jack could spend the afternoon together. Sitting quietly, just content to be in each other's company, they watched as the sun slowly slid across the sky and then finally dipped behind a bank of dark clouds.

A storm was coming.

As Fletcher bowed his head and listened to the rolling thunder, he knew that just as he had lost his wife and daughter, he was on the brink of losing Jack.

He knew that if that happened, then he, too, would be lost.

Lightning, like the snap of a whip, crackled on the horizon.

Fifty

"So that's it, then?" Rogan asked, folding his arms. "There's nothing else we can do?"

"I'm afraid not," Frank replied.

"This isn't right. Have you seen Fletcher lately?"

"I tried to talk to him yesterday, but he's ignoring me. He hasn't spoken to me since our last meeting."

"You know how good he was. You know how much he gave to this war. Why can't they make a goddamn exception on this? The man is teetering on the edge. I've seen it enough to know."

"I've sent special requests right to the top. They feel that if they let Jack come back, there would be no stopping the remaining dog handlers. They're just not prepared to set a precedent. It's too risky for them."

"No one would even know."

Frank shrugged. "What can I say? They aren't prepared to budge."

"This is a fucking travesty."

"I know, but I've done all I can. Believe me. Even ruffled a few feathers in the process. In the end, it all comes down to money. Hell, just about everything does. You could argue that this whole war has been fought over money. About the threat communism poses to capitalism."

Rogan paused as a helicopter swooped overhead. "Do you know that the dog saved my life?"

"I didn't, but I'm not surprised."

"In fact, he saved all of us. And now we're just letting him die?"

"I'm sorry, Rogan. I really am," Frank said, as he packed away the last of his personal effects. "Look, I'm scheduled on the next chopper out. Why don't you join me?"

"No. I'm going to stay with Fletcher and do what I can to make this easier for him."

Frank stood up and held out his hand. "Something that's always impressed me about you, Rogan, is how much you care about your men. You're a fine soldier and a great leader. I hope we get to work together again someday."

"Sure," Rogan sighed, reluctantly shaking his hand, "but next time I'll sit in the office."

Rogan stood at the entrance to the tent and watched as Fletcher brushed Jack.

"He should've died that day," Fletcher said without looking up.

"I'm glad he didn't."

"But he should have."

"Maybe so, but you saved him."

"No. He survived because he was meant to live. I'm convinced of it."

"Fletcher, don't do this. You've done all that you can. You've risked your life for him more than once. You have the strength to get past this—I know it. I've seen it in you."

Fletcher slowly looked up. His eyes were bloodshot and swollen from lack of sleep. "Without Jack, I have nothing left."

"Look, I know you won't be with him, but he might make it out there; he survived before—"

"Alone in this place, he'll be dead in two weeks. Three at the most."

Rogan thought of a reply, but could summon nothing honest. "Everyone's gone, Fletcher. It's just us now. The last chopper will be here any minute. I'll give you some time to say good-bye."

As the lieutenant turned to leave, Fletcher called out to him. "Wait. Hold on, Rogan. Stay . . . *please*."

"If that's what you want."

Fletcher nodded, then lifted Jack up and held him against his chest. "They're taking a register of everyone leaving, aren't they?"

"Yes, why?"

"Will you help me?"

"Of course," Rogan frowned, wondering what Fletcher meant.

Outside, like the sound of a dying heartbeat, one last Huey approached.

Fifty-one

Fletcher Carson? We're under orders to bring you out."

Startled, Fletcher looked up at the two men in military police uniform. They were both armed.

"What's going on?" Rogan asked. "Who ordered this?"

"That's of no concern to you, lieutenant."

"What have you been told?"

"It doesn't concern you," the second soldier repeated. "The bird's waiting. Let's go."

Incensed, Rogan stood up. "Listen, son, you better tell me what the hell's going on right now, or every time you swallow, you're going to be tasting the barrel of that rifle."

The soldier stepped forward, tightening his grip on his M16. "We have orders that do not involve you. Stay out of this. If you don't, we'll be forced to restrain you. Now, let's go."

"Move," his partner chipped in, feeling the need to assert himself.

Fletcher slowly lifted to his feet. Jack, sensing the tension, began to growl.

"Come . . . move out."

As they exited the tent, Fletcher instructed Jack to walk ahead of him. The Labrador's hackles were raised, and he was still growling, but he reluctantly followed Fletcher's command. Outside, the midday heat was even harsher than usual. It was a kind of burning fever that, given enough time, could char a man's flesh. As Fletcher slowed, one of the soldiers nudged him along with his weapon. "Hurry up."

Rogan stopped and turned around. "What's wrong with you men? Why are you doing this?"

"We were told you wouldn't be a problem."

"Look, we're going to get on the damn chopper, but first this man is going to say good-bye to his dog. That's all."

The senior officer shook his head. "We don't have time for that."

Rogan's eyes were wide with rage. "*We don't have time?* Really? Just what the fuck is the big hurry? What the hell's really going on here?"

The soldiers exchanged looks.

"We have orders to shoot the dog," the senior officer replied.

"No . . . please!" Fletcher called out.

"Stand aside, Carson," the officer instructed, raising his rifle for the first time.

Fletcher knelt down and shepherded Jack behind him. "You'll have to shoot me first."

"Spare me the dramatics. It's only a goddamn dog."

Detecting Fletcher's resolve, the soldiers fanned out to create an angle for a shot. As Rogan stepped forward to help Fletcher, the second officer screamed at him. "Stay where you are!"

"Stop this, please," Fletcher urged.

"Make this easier on yourself, Carson . . . Move aside."

Fletcher tried to spread himself over Jack, but the officer fired a shot anyway. The bullet narrowly missed him.

"Have you lost your minds?" Rogan shouted. "You're going to kill him!"

"Then order your man to move away from the dog now!"

The situation had spiraled out of control. Fletcher knew he had to do something drastic. With his mind racing, he grabbed a handful of sand and hurled it in the face of the senior officer.

Instinctively, the man dropped his rifle and brought his hands up to his eyes. The incident distracted his partner, and he inadvertently shifted his rifle away from Rogan for an instant. It was a minor lapse, but all the gap Rogan needed. He lunged forward and punched the soldier. The blow might've killed him outright had it not glanced off the side of his jaw. It was still powerful enough to send him crashing to the ground. Rogan quickly disarmed him and ran across to Fletcher, who was wrestling with the senior officer. "Let him go."

The officer stopped resisting, and Fletcher pulled his rifle off him. He shoved the barrel under the man's chin. "How does it feel, you piece of shit?"

Jack, with his hackles raised, was standing at Fletcher's side, waiting for an attack command. He was barely able to restrain himself.

"Easy, Fletcher," Rogan said. "He isn't worth it."

But Fletcher was in another place. A world filled with anger and death. Where loss and despair walked arm in arm and all those he loved kept being taken away from him. "Why shouldn't I kill you? Answer me! *Answer me, you fuck!*"

"Because I'll take down your lieutenant," a voice intruded from behind them.

It was the pilot. With the sound of the rotors disguising his movements, he had managed to sneak up behind them undetected. He was standing only five feet behind Rogan with his sidearm drawn. "Enough of this shit. Lower your weapons, both of you."

The scene had become surreal to Fletcher. "I just want you to let my dog go."

"Return the rifle to the officer and get on the chopper."

"Will you let my dog live?"

"Put down your weapon and get on the fucking bird!"

Fletcher was out of options. He sensed the pilot was willing to fire if pressed. Rogan had already sacrificed enough for him; he couldn't endanger his life any further—this wasn't his burden to bear. He took a deep breath and turned to look at Jack. "Ruush," he whispered, fighting back the tears. *"Ruuush."*

It was the command for Jack to run.

It had taken them a long time to teach it to him, as he never felt comfortable leaving them. It simply went against his nature.

Jack looked back at him as if he'd been given the wrong command.

"Ruush, Jack, now. *Please.*"

The emotion in Fletcher's voice only served to add to Jack's confusion. He took two steps back, then stopped. *"Jack!"* Fletcher lifted the rifle away from the officer's neck and fired a shot next to the Labrador.

Jack's eyes darted between the rifle and where the bullet had skipped off the ground.

Fletcher felt like his heart was being pulled out of his chest.

"Run, Jacky . . . run . . . please . . . They're going to kill you," he cried, firing more rounds into the ground. "Ruush!"

Reluctantly, Jack turned and fled.

"Let my dog run," Fletcher screamed, pressing the rifle into the back of the officer's head, "or I will take the life from this man. Do not fucking test me!"

As Jack disappeared from view, Fletcher waited a moment before discarding the rifle and stepping back. The senior officer, angered and embarrassed to have lost control of the situation, quickly retrieved his weapon and swung it at Fletcher. Blood exploded from his forehead.

"Leave him alone, you bastard!"

"Shut up!" the young officer screamed, reclaiming his own weapon.

The pilot turned away and headed back to the helicopter. "Get them on board and put restraints on them. Think you two can handle that?"

The senior officer yanked Fletcher to his feet. "Just give me a reason to kill you. In the chopper, now!"

As they moved, Rogan turned to Fletcher. "You all right?"

Blood was streaming down his face, soaking the front of his white shirt. "This wasn't supposed to happen. This wasn't the plan . . ."

"What plan? What're you talking about?"

But Fletcher didn't respond. Something in his mind had finally let go.

They were pushed on board and forced to lie down on their stomachs with their arms held behind them. While the officers searched for handcuffs, the pilot fired up the chopper.

As they lay together, facing each other, Rogan spoke again. "What do you mean 'this wasn't part of the plan'?"

Fletcher could only shake his head.

"Fletcher! What plan are you talking about?" Rogan insisted as the helicopter lifted off.

"You said you would help me," Fletcher uttered. "Please . . . *help me.*" He lifted his head and stared intensely at Rogan. "I can't leave him behind."

Rogan looked at him blankly for a moment, and then suddenly understood what he wanted. "But you'll die."

Fletcher shook his head. "I'll die anyway."

Reluctantly, Rogan nodded. He held Fletcher's gaze for a moment before turning over and, in one fluid movement, tackling the two soldiers into the back of the pilot's seat.

Fletcher pulled himself to the edge of the cabin. The chopper was rising steeply. Out of the corner of his eye, he saw movement.

It was Jack.

He was running after the helicopter.

Just as Fletcher had stepped off a ledge to end his life months before, he again plunged into another abyss. Except this time, he was falling to save himself. As he plummeted to the ground, he felt himself turning over. He landed on his back with his leg buckled underneath him. A sudden jolt of pain drove through his spine. He struggled onto his haunches just as Jack reached him. The Labrador launched himself into his arms.

He held him close, and Jack licked the side of his face. "I was never going to leave you. I never planned to get on that chopper. Never . . . never . . ."

The helicopter hovered above them, and Fletcher watched as the two officers battled to subdue Rogan. Before they overpowered him, he managed to get hold of a gun and push it out of the cabin.

Then, just as Fletcher had suspected, instead of landing and trying to reapprehend him, the helicopter continued to rise. For them, the war was over. One more lost soldier with a suicide wish meant nothing in their lives. As he watched the helicopter disappear, Rogan, who was still being kicked and punched, managed to stretch his arm out the cabin. He pressed his thumb into the palm of his hand and extended two fingers. It was one of the many dog commands they had taught Jack.

It meant *find home.*

PART II

Left Behind

Fifty-two

Fletcher sat holding Jack until he could no longer hear the chopper.

As his breathing eased and he checked himself to make sure nothing was broken, his mind turned to Rogan. He could barely believe what his lieutenant had done for him. His actions would have dire consequences back home. He would almost certainly face a court-martial, perhaps even jail time. His career in the army was all but over.

"Thank you, lieutenant," Fletcher whispered, staring up into the sky. "For everything."

Jack shifted in his arms and nuzzled his hand.

"Sorry if I scared you, buddy."

Jack blinked at him and then rested his chin on Fletcher's leg. He was just happy that they were together again.

"Christ. It's just us now, Jack. Alone in hell."

Fletcher lifted to his feet and scanned the deserted base. It was an eerie scene.

There was a dreamlike quality about it. Half a dozen of the older tents remained, as well as two permanent supply rooms and an empty munitions depot, but without the constant throng of soldiers, it felt like a foreign landscape. Like visiting an amusement park after closing time, a menacing air had settled over the place.

"Surplus military equipment," he remarked cynically before moving toward the tent closest to them. It was a dark, depressing space that had been used predominantly for briefings and tactical sessions, and brought back bad memories for him. He walked inside and headed to the far corner of the room. He knelt down and began to dig through the soft sand.

A moment later, he pulled out a map and compass wrapped in a clear plastic bag.

"I told you I never meant to get on that chopper."

Jack tilted his head and tried to bite the bag.

Fletcher had never intended to abandon Jack. Although a last resort, an ambitious contingency plan had been lingering in the back of his mind for some time. The arrival of the two MPs, however, almost derailed his plan. Unfolding the map, he used his finger to trace a line from their base westward, out of Vietnam, across Laos, and into Thailand—a country friendly to the United States. The route constituted some 350 miles of hostile territory.

He looked down at Jack and smiled, but there was a darkness clouding his expression. "I know what you're thinking, but we can do this."

They were going to hike out of Vietnam.

Fifty-three

The Strip had been one of the last U.S. bases to pull out of the central region of Vietnam. There wasn't another American soul for almost 150 miles. Not that it mattered anymore. Fletcher had no intention of traveling south. They were going to head west: directly through Laos and into Thailand. There he would find a way to get them home. A 350-mile walk on an open road would take upwards of ten days. Their journey was more likely to take a month, perhaps even longer.

With Jack following closely behind, Fletcher began to gather the supplies he had stowed away. After a few minutes, he sat down and assessed their stockpile. In total, there were four water canisters, two boxes of matches, two loaves of bread, sixteen soup powders, and a pile of exactly 157 dog biscuits. The water canisters were extremely important because although there were likely to be numerous water sources along their route, not all of it would be safe to drink. Coupled with the heat and the fact that they were at the end of the rainy season, dehydration would be a major concern.

Their biscuits would become their staple diet, by far their most nutritious food source. They could survive on a handful of them a day, provided they supplemented their diet with whatever else they could source from the jungle. In his initial training, Fletcher had been lectured briefly on basic survival skills, but at the time of his enlistment, the war's demand for fresh troops superseded the need for thorough instruction. In practice, anyway, the length of their assignments had never tested their proficiency on jungle survival, and he had already forgotten much of what there was to know. He had tried to pry some information from some of the more experienced soldiers on base, but few could offer any useful advice. Most of their knowledge was limited to the obvious fruits, rice, sugarcane, and a few roots that offered some nutritional value. Mitchell would have been the ideal person to ask, but the question would have made him suspicious. Despite this, Fletcher was reasonably confident of his basic survival knowledge—provided the Laos vegetation didn't differ too much from Vietnam. If things got desperate, he could always hunt for food using the gun Rogan had thrown out of the chopper, but at the risk of bringing unwanted attention to themselves, it would be only as a last resort.

After picking up an old, worn rucksack, Fletcher loaded their supplies. He wondered what their chances of survival were. Apart from the sheer physical demands of the trip, they would have to negotiate traps and pass undetected for weeks. His navigating would also have to be extremely accurate. Laos may not have seen as much fighting as Vietnam, but it was still decidedly hostile territory. It was also home to Charlie's largest supply route to the South—the infamous Ho Chi Minh trail—which he would have to traverse in the days that followed. Passing by unnoticed was going to be a major undertaking.

As he loaded some of the biscuits into a pocket on the side of the rucksack, he felt a small bulge near the bottom. He reached down and withdrew the object. It was a small first aid kit. Inside were scissors, bandages, a needle, a length of surgeon's thread, and three small vials of penicillin. It was an important find. Jack pushed his nose into the plastic tub and sniffed its contents.

"Let's hope we don't need this."

That night, like most nights, Fletcher battled to fall asleep. The Strip, which had been their sanctuary for so long, was now a dangerous place to be. It felt like an open wound exposed to infection. There was no question that Charlie would be coming soon—sweeping through the deserted camps like scavengers picking at the wet bones of a rotting corpse. Just not tonight, Fletcher hoped.

He had chosen a small tent close to a bank of trees so that if Charlie did arrive during the course of the night, they might still be able to slip away unnoticed. Fortunately, the soldiers wouldn't be expecting anyone to be left on base and would likely make a fair bit of noise as they approached. After settling down, they quickly shared half a loaf of bread and two of the soups, but Fletcher was still hungry.

Earlier, he had found a six-pack of beer and was tempted to have one, but knew that he would pay for it later. Alcohol would dehydrate him, and that was something he could ill afford. To survive, they would have to think very carefully about every single decision they made: The slightest mistake, he knew, could be fatal.

Eventually, after focusing his mind on the sound of Jack's steady breathing, Fletcher fell into a deep sleep.

Thankfully, his nightmares stayed away.

Fifty-four

"Who's there?" Fletcher mumbled, startled. He had no idea what had woken him, only that something felt wrong. The front flap of the tent swayed gently in the breeze. As he leaned forward to push it open, a shadow appeared on the canvas wall beside him. He snatched at his gun. The figure was stooped over, but the pose seemed exaggerated.

"*Jesus,* Jack," he said as the Labrador poked his head inside the tent. "Where've you been?"

Jack wagged his tail and flopped down with half his body still left outside.

"Don't get too comfortable." He yawned, noticing the darkness beginning to lift on the horizon. "It's almost time for us to go."

Setting the gun back down, he ran his fingers over the stubble that now covered his head. He had gotten up in the middle of the night and, partly inspired by a dream he was having, decided to shave his head in an attempt to pass for one of the few Buddhists in the area. The thought, he knew, first germinated when he had stumbled onto an old brown robe while collecting their supplies. It was remarkably similar to those worn by the Buddhists. He hoped that the clothing, combined with his subtle Asian features, would be convincing enough. It couldn't hurt to try. After all, there was no logical reason for a U.S. soldier to be disguising himself as a Buddhist monk, not at this point of the war, anyway. If anything would give him away, however, it would be his height. In America, he was only slightly above average height; in Vietnam, he was a virtual giant.

As the sky continued to lighten, Fletcher's anxiety grew. The farthest he had ever hiked was seventy miles over six days. Their journey ahead was five times that. Trying to ready himself, he scanned the abandoned base and was suddenly unnerved at how quiet it was. There were no jeeps. No Hueys. No voices. There was nothing.

Just them, alone in the enemy's garden. Forsaken.

Fifty-five

The first four days were mercifully uneventful. With the war over, there were very few active patrols left in the area. They encountered Charlie only once, and even then, he appeared more concerned about being snared in one of his own traps than anything else—a concern Fletcher shared. Twice Jack had sniffed out trip wires that he had missed. On both occasions, it had been late in the day. Fletcher found that his concentration began to waver after about nine hours. Jack's mind, however, seemed never to tire, as if attuned to the marathon demands of their journey.

They had been walking most of the afternoon when Fletcher noticed an old wooden sign lying facedown in the mud ahead of them. After inspecting it to make sure it wasn't wired to a grenade, he carefully pried it up with his knife.

A large part of its message had long since been scrubbed away by the wind and the rain, but a portion survived.

LAOS.

It confirmed what he had been hoping. Sometime during the day, they had crossed over the border. By his calculations, they had already covered more than sixty miles. He was overjoyed at how quickly they had progressed, but was also wary of their pace. During the last few hours, Jack had developed a slight limp. It was barely noticeable, but it was definitely there. He had been walking behind Jack long enough to tell when something was wrong. After checking the paw to ensure he hadn't picked up a thorn, he thought the injury related back to the shooting and worried what condition the Labrador would be in a week from now, a month from now.

Stopping for a moment, Fletcher laid Jack down and stretched out his back legs. He pressed his hand down gently on the scar above his hip, and Jack yipped in pain.

"All right, Jack, all right. We'll slow down tomorrow. Take things a little easier for a while."

He had planned for them to do at least another mile before sundown, but thought better of it. Jack needed to rest. Checking the area, he found a well-covered spot near the base of a large tree, where they could spend the night. As always, he climbed the tree to get a better look at their surroundings. Most times, the dense vegetation prevented him from seeing farther than a hundred yards or so, but it made him feel better to try.

Satisfied, he opened the rucksack and took out their food for the evening. Three dog biscuits each and a packet of soup to share. They hadn't had soup since their first night.

"Tonight we eat like kings, Jack," he announced, carefully tearing open the packet. He unscrewed one of the canteens and splashed some water into a small plastic container. He mixed the powder with his knife, then took three generous sips. He put the rest down for Jack. The soup would have tasted a good deal more appetizing had they been able to heat it, but they couldn't afford the attention a fire would bring.

They chased down the soup with the biscuits and a few mouthfuls of fresh water.

Dinner took all of three minutes to prepare and consume.

"I'll never take any food for granted again, that's for sure."

Jack moved alongside Fletcher and, as always, rested his head on his thigh.

"Get some sleep, Jack. We've got a long way to go. We're barely down the driveway."

If the Vietnam day was a full song, its dusk was a single note.

In a beat, it was gone.

Fifty-six

Day 7

Jack's limp was now becoming a serious issue. It had deteriorated from a slight hobble to the point where his back right paw would touch down on the ground only every third or fourth stride. As troubling as it was, it didn't slow him much—not yet, at least. They were still able to maintain the kind of pace that, one week into their journey, was surprisingly efficient.

Over the past two days, however, Fletcher's legs had started to cramp from the mileage. His calves, in particular, were locking up every few hours. Each attack would force them to stop so that Fletcher could massage out the spasm. The whole process delayed them for around ten minutes at a time. A worrying sign was that the intervals between the cramps were getting smaller, and their grip lasting longer.

The physical exertion was only part of the reason for the cramping. The rest was down to their diet.

Fletcher had stowed away a large packet of salt under a board in the munitions depot, which would have dealt with much of the cramping, but he had forgotten to retrieve it before leaving. It was an oversight, he knew, that could have serious consequences for them—particularly as they entered the second half of their journey.

On the positive side, they had managed to safely cross over the infamous Ho Chi Minh trail, which was more like a superhighway cutting through the jungle than the quaint walking path its name implied. It stretched for hundreds of kilometers from the north of Vietnam, down the Chaine Annamitique mountains in Laos, and back into the south of Vietnam. It included a massive pipeline that supplied Charlie with all the fuel he needed and was a key channel for small trucks, bicycles, and elephants ferrying tons of equipment and supplies. The trail had been Charlie's lifeblood. During the height of the war, a constant flow of traffic traversed its spine. Without it, the Vietnam conflict might well have been a different proposition altogether.

Fletcher wished the trail led to Thailand. That way, they might have been able to stow away on the back of a truck. But they were heading west while the trail was winding south. Bisecting the path meant that they had covered something in the region of a hundred miles. It was an important milestone for them, but still two thirds of their journey lay ahead of them. He had expected to face heavy traffic on the trail, but in the few minutes while they waited in the surrounding brush, they encountered only a solitary truck and a convoy of three motorbikes.

So far, so good.

Nightfall brought with it welcome rain. After days of clear skies, Fletcher celebrated its arrival. Following the natural path of the water as it flowed through the trees and funneled down leaves, he carefully positioned their water canisters until they were full to the brim.

Making the most of the situation, they both drank until their stomachs were bloated.

The water was soft and delicious; every sip was savored.

Fletcher filled and refilled their plastic container three times for Jack. Despite an almost insatiable thirst, Fletcher was mindful of overhydration—a condition he knew could be fatal. Of all the things that could kill them, it would be almost a parody to succumb to too much fresh water; he had to fight his instincts to drink more.

Using a thin ground sheet to shelter them from the downpour, Fletcher watched as the rain pooled at their feet. He had been truly grateful for the shower, as fresh water had been more difficult to source than he had expected, but now his thoughts turned to where they would hole up for the night. The prospect of sleeping in the mud was becoming more and more likely by the minute.

The wet jungle was a bouquet of smells, dominated by a rich blend of minerals and irons that rose up from the soil. Whether it was the driving rain or just a simple lapse in concentration, Fletcher didn't see the animal until it was right on top of them.

He stared straight into its eyes, less than ten feet away, but still couldn't believe what he was seeing.

The animal was stalking them. Hunting them.

It seemed impossible. *Am I hallucinating?* he wondered.

The predator's orange stripes, like licks of flame, lit up the gloom.

Fifty-seven

Fletcher slowly withdrew his sidearm, mindful of making any sudden, threatening movements. The tiger crouched down, the muscles in its shoulders writhing and contorting like snakes coiling under a silk sheet. Its variegated coat appeared almost fluorescent in the pouring rain. The last thing Fletcher wanted to do was shoot it. He sensed the animal was desperate and hadn't eaten in some time. They were not known to hunt humans, but it was clearly hungry. Jack let out a low, threatening growl, and Fletcher quickly grabbed his collar to stop him from committing what would have amounted to canine suicide.

The tiger, as big as a small car, took a half step forward, as if testing the waters ahead of it. It was now within striking range.

Fletcher cocked his gun.

He had heard of wild tigers roaming through Southeast Asia, but had never seen one. "Find something else, friend," he said in a deep, steady voice.

The animal glanced down at the gun as if it had only just noticed the weapon, and took a step back. Clearly it had been burned by a hot barrel before. Exploiting its fear, Fletcher waved the pistol around in a slow arc. "That's it . . . move away."

The tiger stood its ground at first, but then slowly backtracked through the trees. Then, just as suddenly as it had appeared, it vanished.

"Did that really just happen?" Fletcher asked, easing his grip on Jack's collar. The Labrador's hackles were raised like quills.

"I think it's gone. Jesus, I hope so."

But for how long? he wondered. Would it return later while they slept? As unlikely as that might have been, he wasn't taking any chances. They would have to find somewhere relatively safe to rest. And safety, in this context, meant up a tree.

Most of the trees in the area were patently unsuitable. They were either too thin or their branches weren't conducive to sleeping on. To add to their woes, the driving rain had brought about an early dusk. Soon it would be too dark to continue their search, and they would be forced to spend the night awake.

"Come on, give us a break," Fletcher pleaded, scanning the trees in the distance. "We need the goddamn rest."

Dejected, he took a deep breath, and as he did, something flickered in the bottom of his vision. He cupped his hands over his eyes and leaned forward.

Was it metal? Glass?

At first, he thought his eyes were deceiving him, but as he moved closer, his doubts evaporated. The shell of a small truck, stripped bare of its wheels and engine, was wedged in between two tall trees.

"How the hell did that get here?" He laughed, striding out toward it. He stepped up to the driver's door and was about to open it, when he realized it might be booby-trapped. After satisfying himself that it wasn't rigged to anything that might violently liberate his limbs from his torso, he carefully clicked it open.

He felt like crying.

All the windows were intact, and the front seat bench—a worn-down beige mattress, really—was big enough for both of them to stretch out on. "It's like the goddamn Ritz!" he cheered. "C'mon, Jack . . . get in."

Once inside, Fletcher stripped off his wet clothes and used a small towel to dry Jack's coat. Within minutes, all the windows had misted up. The harder it rained, the less likely it was that they would be found. They were dry and warm, and Fletcher couldn't help but feel that they were safe, enveloped in a protected cocoon.

Real or not, it was a wonderful feeling.

Overcome, he suddenly felt like singing, but the impulse soon passed. The only song worthy of the moment did not belong exclusively to him. It was Kingston's first and the Fat Lady's second. He was just a member of that choir—a group that had long since disbanded. Alone, the song would have no soul.

Fifty-eight

Day 15

After the cramp had eased, Fletcher removed his socks and wrung out the sweat, which was now tinged red with blood. The coppery stench made him feel nauseated. He wished he could at least wash his hands, scrub them, to get rid of the dried blood that was caked under his fingernails, but it was a luxury they could ill afford. He looked down in dismay at his feet. Although not quite raw, they were covered in thin cuts and blisters. He had already lost two toenails, and two more were threatening to peel away. His right heel was cracked, and a similar chasm was beginning to open on his left foot.

Jack wasn't faring any better. His troublesome back right leg was now a useless appendage. He was reduced to dragging it behind him, no longer able to hold it up. As a result, the hair on top of his paw had been worn away and replaced by a thin wet scab.

Infection had already set in; Fletcher could smell it. Following much deliberation, he decided to administer two vials of their precious penicillin to Jack. He couldn't afford to allow the infection to persist.

After he was done, he strapped up the paw with a torn section of his shirt. "There, Jack, that should help you along."

They were both in some pain, but of more immediate concern was their food reserves, which had dwindled far quicker than Fletcher originally calculated. They were down to just three soups and fifty-seven biscuits.

Not nearly enough to sustain them, given the energy they were expending.

A less worrisome, but remarkably odd thing was happening to Fletcher. His hair was falling out. When he rubbed the top of his head, his hand would be covered in hundreds of short hairs. It was more damning evidence of their lack of proper nutrition.

He forced his shoes back on and winced as he tightened the laces. Standing up was always the worst. He had to put his hands on his knees to steady himself. The pain brought on another powerful wave of nausea, which he had to contain at all costs. If he vomited, he would lose the little food he had just eaten and, with it, what remained of his strength.

Another afternoon of agony lay ahead of them, and there was no time to waste. Jack waited until Fletcher started moving again before trotting up to point. As ever, he was searching and sniffing for danger. Since entering Laos, there had been a noticeable decline in traps; while the country had been active in the war, it had not been on the same scale as Vietnam. Complacency, more than anything, was their biggest enemy now.

Surprisingly, the more they walked, the better Fletcher felt. Each step was half a yard closer to Thailand.

Closer to home.

The pain seemed to numb after an hour until all that was left was a sense of heaviness at the bottom of his legs. That, and the faint sensation of sweat and blood squelching between his toes.

Although they ate more than he had planned, Fletcher suspected they walked farther, as well. By nightfall, he calculated they would have covered over 250 miles. Only one hundred miles to go. He was starting to believe.

Fifty-nine

Day 20

Another impossibly dark night in Laos. Despite the lack of cloud cover, the jungle was a myriad of overlapping shadows, as if the air itself was blackened smoke. During the first few nights, the darkness had been oppressive. Now, it felt comfortable, like the company of an old friend. Fletcher had become used to functioning without light and was no longer perturbed by the insects that occasionally wandered over his body. For the most part, they were harmless. Those that weren't were apt to act only if their own lives were threatened. Even snakes, and there had been many, barely factored on his list of things that were likely to harm them. As for stings, well . . . he barely felt them anymore.

What was of growing concern, however, was a painful and disturbing throbbing that had burrowed into the lower half of his legs.

His feet had become so swollen that to take off his shoes, he had to remove his shoelaces.

Jack was in worse shape.

Using the canvas sheet to conceal the light, Fletcher shone his torch onto Jack's bandaged paw. He needed to change the dressing. As he unfurled the dirty rag, the smell that emerged made his eyes water. The wound was covered in a thick, murky layer of slime and blood. The skin around the area was tight and swollen. He unscrewed the lid from one of the water canisters and poured it over the wound. As he gently prodded the area, he could feel there was a severe buildup of fluid under the skin. He immediately unpacked his knife and a box of matches and began to burn the tip of the blade. After a few seconds, when the steel was an angry black, he tightened his grip around the top of Jack's leg.

"This is going to hurt, but I promise you'll feel better afterwards."

He pushed the knife into the middle of Jack's paw, and a thick wave of pus splashed up onto the blade.

Jack whimpered and tried to withdraw his leg. When he couldn't, he licked the side of Fletcher's arm.

"I know it hurts, buddy, but we have to do this."

Although some of the buildup had cleared, Fletcher knew the worst was still to come. When he traced his fingers over the wound, he could feel other underlying pockets of fluid and firmer areas where the pus had hardened. As Fletcher pushed the blade into a new area, Jack latched on to the back of his arm but didn't bite down.

Under no circumstances would he ever harm Fletcher.

That morning they waited an hour after sunrise before moving. They both needed the extra rest. Fletcher was relieved to see that the swelling in Jack's paw had gone down noticeably. As a reward for enduring the lancing, Fletcher mixed a bowl of their penultimate packet of soup and gave it all to Jack.

He needed the extra energy to fight off the infection, anyway.

Fletcher thought of taking off his boots to check on his feet, but decided against it. He had a good enough idea of how they looked. Instead, he loosened his laces a fraction to give his feet at least some room to move.

"C'mon, Jack. Another week of this crap, and we'll be in Thailand. From there . . . somehow I'll find us a way home."

Jack rose slowly and wagged his tail. He stepped forward and managed to touch the ground with his injured paw. He quickly lifted it up as if he had trodden on a hot coal, but it was a definite sign of improvement.

Given their situation, even the smallest victories were worth celebrating. With that as their inspiration, they pressed forward. Another day of hobbling through the jungle beckoned.

Sixty

As the afternoon shadows lengthened, Fletcher felt increasingly detached from their situation. His head felt light and dizzy. He had also begun to lose sensation in his legs, which wasn't, he felt, an entirely bad thing. His arms tingled from the elbows down. He had to constantly refer to the map and compass to ensure they remained on the correct heading, but was finding it difficult to concentrate on their coordinates. At one stage, he found himself at the top of a steep slope with no memory of how he got there. Long passages of time were now unaccounted for.

But that wasn't the worst of it.

Paranoia, like an insidious disease, was starting to creep under his skin. Suddenly Charlie was everywhere: hiding in the grass, waiting behind bushes, stalking him from behind. Twice, he almost shot at trees, convinced soldiers were hiding behind them.

The lines between reality and delirium were starting to blur. Periods of lucidity served only to add to his confusion.

And then the dead started showing up.

He first saw the two officers he had assassinated in the tunnel complex sitting peacefully in a tree, fresh blood still seeping from their wounds. Then the first man he had killed in Vietnam—a young, barefoot soldier with a spider tattoo on his neck—appeared through the jungle ahead of him. A female soldier he'd shot in the hand suddenly leapt out at him, waving her torn appendage in his direction.

He couldn't take it anymore. He stopped walking and dropped to his knees. For the first time, he noticed how thick and swollen his tongue was. He was barely able to swallow. He opened one of the water canisters and took a long sip, but it did little more than bring on another tide of nausea. He poured the remaining contents of the bottle into Jack's bowl. As he listened to him drink, Fletcher lay down.

"I have to rest, Jack," he heard himself whisper. "I'm just so . . . *tired* . . ."

Suddenly, he was exhausted. It felt like they had walked halfway across the world. He just needed to stop for a while.

To close his eyes.

Get his shit together.

Just for a minute.

A kick.

At least that's what it felt like. Fletcher tried to open his eyes, but the late afternoon sun was blinding. There were several dark figures crowded around him.

Was he still hallucinating?

Dreaming?

He tried to talk, but one of the figures rammed something into his face. This was no dream; the pain was excruciating. It felt like the side of his head had caved in. As he struggled to his feet, loud voices shouted at him.

Another strike to his head. Then one against his back.

The onslaught took his breath away. He tried to raise his arms to defend himself, but the back of his hand was violently swatted down by what felt like the butt of a rifle. He felt and then heard the bones crack.

As his vision narrowed, he heard Jack attack one of the men. From the sound of the man's cries, he was being torn to pieces.

"Please leave my dog. Please!" Fletcher shouted, collapsing to the ground, "Jack . . . *ruush* . . . ruush . . . get out of here!"

But Jack was trying to defend him.

As if a powerful anesthetic were coursing through his veins, Fletcher felt his world begin to recede. But just before its blackness was drawn over him, he was afforded one final sight. It would break him in every way that a man could be broken.

A soldier smashed the side of his rifle into Jack's face, spun it around, and as an early twilight fell, carrying Fletcher away, two shots were fired.

Sixty-one

Day 23

Fletcher woke up with a start.

"Easy mate," a voice issued from behind him. "You're pretty banged up. Been out for some time now."

He was lying on a hard mud floor. His head was wrapped in a strip of green material, and he was sweating profusely.

"You're bloody lucky to be alive."

"Where am I?" he managed, his throat struggling to manufacture the words.

"The end of the line, I suppose."

Fletcher blinked through the fog in his eyes and tried to absorb his surroundings. The prison was no bigger than six or seven square yards and made entirely from thick bamboo struts bound together by heavy wire. Through the space between the bars, he could see five or six bungalows in the distance. There was a lookout tower some eighty yards away, on top of which two guards were sharing a cigarette. The area around him stank of urine and feces.

"What's your name, friend?" The voice belonged to a tall bearded man with a mane of curly blond hair. His accent was unmistakably Australian.

"Fletcher," he offered. "How long have I been here?"

"A couple of days."

"Where are we?" he asked again, praying they weren't back in Vietnam.

"We're in a prison camp about forty miles out of Cambodia."

"Still in Laos."

"Yeah."

"How far from—?"

"Thailand? About fifty-five miles east, I reckon," he said, then laughed. "But we may as well be on another planet."

As the man spoke, Fletcher's thoughts turned immediately to Jack. He recalled, all too vividly, seeing the Labrador hit in the face and hearing two shots fired. The image scalded him like a branding iron. Had Jack been killed?

He had to have been; the shots were fired at such close range.

How could he have fallen asleep? Fletcher thought suddenly, furious with himself.

It was all his fault.

He had failed Jack.

"Tell me . . ." Fletcher said, clearing his throat. "When they brought me in, did you see if they were carrying a dog?"

"A dog? What . . . yours?"

"Yes."

"Why would they bring your dog back with you?"

Fletcher's reply was barely audible. "For food. Please, do you remember seeing anything?"

The man stared at the ground. "I saw them bring you in straight through the entrance to the camp, and I'm pretty sure they weren't carrying a dog."

Hope, like the vague warmth of a sunrise, lifted Fletcher. If Jack had been killed, there was a strong likelihood the soldiers would've brought his body back to camp. Then again, perhaps he was reaching.

"Look, I know it's none of my business, but I've got to ask you something," the Australian said. "The war ended weeks ago, but you've only just arrived here. Where the hell have you been?"

Fletcher looked down at his feet and noticed that his legs were tied to one of the thick bamboo struts. "We were," he began, his voice drifting away, "on our way home."

Sixty-two

In the days following his capture, Fletcher clung to the slim hope that Jack was still alive; he had little choice but to do so. He was simply not willing to contemplate the alternative. He had forged a comfortable bond with the Australian, Matthew Summers, which he knew was largely fueled by their shared circumstances. They debated, at length, different ways of escaping, but despite some promising ideas, they had not yet come up with a plausible plan. Fletcher learned that there had been another soldier in the cage, but shortly before his arrival, the man had been dragged down to the river alongside them, given the beating of his life, and shot in the head. So far, he himself had been questioned three times by their captors. They were more than a little curious as to why an American soldier was traveling on his own in the middle of Laos. They suspected he was on a reconnaissance mission of sorts. Neither of the beatings lasted more than an hour. In each case, Fletcher refused to utter even a single word. By the end of the week, they began to lose interest in reshaping his face.

After a fourth beating revealed nothing, they sent him back to his cage for good. Fletcher knew that the next time they came for him, it would be to put a bullet in his head.

Until that day arrived, he spent much of his time replaying the moment of his capture over in his mind. Was it really possible that Jack was still alive? Had he maybe been shot, but escaped? Was he lying in the jungle somewhere slowly bleeding to death? As these dark thoughts and others connected to them continued to plague him, a soldier in his early twenties approached them carrying two tin cups. For reasons Fletcher had not been able to fathom, the young man had been surprisingly kind to them and particularly friendly to him. He had given them extra food and, instead of river water, had twice brought them warm soup.

The soldier carefully pushed the cups inside the cage and backed away. "Drink tea. Get better. You see. You see!"

It was the same four sentences from the day before.

"War over. Soon you go home."

This was new.

"No," Matthew replied, pressing his finger against his temple. "Soon we go dead."

The young soldier shook his head. "No . . . war finish . . . no more dead! Home soon for everyone!"

"Thanks, mate, but they're going to kill us. Trust me."

The soldier knelt down and tried to get Fletcher's attention. "You feel better? Is tea help?"

Fletcher stared at the young man, then slowly nodded. "Tea help very much. Thank you for your kindness."

A smile dawned on the man's face. He was pleased to finally draw out a reaction from Fletcher.

"I bring more tea?"

Fletcher held up his hand. "No. We have enough."

"More food?"

The soldier's keenness to help was becoming more of a mystery by the minute.

"More food is good," Matthew offered.

The soldier quickly rose to his feet and ran off. Within minutes, he returned with a large wooden bowl brimming with rice.

It was more food than Fletcher had seen in days.

As Matthew accepted the bowl and began scooping handfuls into his mouth, Fletcher reached out through the bars and gently grabbed the young man's arm. "What's your name?"

The man regarded Fletcher warily for a moment, wondering if perhaps he was about to be pulled against the bars and strangled. "My name Lee. Lee Tao."

"I'm Fletcher, and this is Matthew. Why are you helping us?"

The soldier leaned in closer to the cage. "You not remember?"

"Remember what?"

"Small village near Suang. You save us!"

For a moment, Fletcher had no idea what he was talking about, but then a gossamer memory—flimsy and delicate—floated across his mind.

During one of their assignments several months ago, they had come across a small village that Charlie was tormenting. Several of the young girls had been raped as the Vietcong continued to intimidate and forcibly recruit able-bodied young men into their army. Those who refused were murdered in plain view, butchered mostly, and their wives and children beaten. Even the elderly were attacked. As it happened, the Fat Lady decided to wait for this particular band of soldiers who were due back the following morning to recruit more of the men. As Charlie marched arrogantly into the village shortly after daybreak, intent on more bloodletting, the Fat Lady was waiting for them. The firefight lasted less than a minute. It was the only time Fletcher had ever extracted any joy in taking another man's life—so much so, in fact, that he took four of them.

"More men returned after we left, didn't they? That's why you're here."

"They very angry. My wife . . . they were going kill her," Lee explained.

"I'm sorry. How long have you been here?"

"Five months," he answered, then glanced over his shoulder to make sure no one was watching their protracted conversation. "Please tell me . . . is village okay? Is my wife still alive?"

"I don't know. I'm very sorry, Lee."

Lee's expression darkened. "Eat food . . . Mr. Fletcher. I see you tomorrow." With that, he stood up and ran toward the bungalows.

As he watched him go, Fletcher realized just how futile their war effort had been. They had helped protect Lee's village once, but Charlie was always going to return. His will was unyielding. In the end, the ghost had been unstoppable.

Sixty-three

The next morning, Fletcher woke up with a fever and an almost debilitating headache that bordered on a migraine. He was sure it wasn't malaria, but rather a nasty dose of flu. Rubbing his eyes, which now felt like swollen marbles, he tried to swallow and discovered that he could now add a raging throat infection to his growing list of ailments.

"No offense, Fletcher, but you look like shit."

"It's my new diet plan." His voice cracked and he rolled gingerly onto his side. "But it's not for everyone."

"You've been out since early last night. I was beginning to think you'd never wake up."

"I've been conserving my energy. I was thinking of crawling to your side of the cage today."

Matthew smiled. "And why would you want to do that?"

"Change of scenery. Also I'm not crazy about my current neighbor; maybe I'll have better luck on your side."

"I thought you said you were a writer not a comedian?"

Fletcher managed a smirk. "Any idea what time it is?"

"Must be around eight. The sun's been up for hours already."

"Christ, it's so fucking hot in here," Fletcher replied. He didn't think he could face another day in their bamboo keep.

"I wonder what's keeping our friend this morning. He's late," Matthew said.

"I think he might be in some trouble for yesterday. I doubt we'll see him again."

Matthew carved his initials in the sand with a small stick. He alternated between that and the Australian flag. "I hope you're wrong."

"Yeah, me too."

"It's a good thing you helped out his village. These things all happen for a reason, you know."

"Lucky coincidence, that's all."

"You think so? I think it's karma. You defended him and his wife, and now you're being repaid."

"I don't believe much in that type of thing. If it does exist, you have to wonder what kind of sick shit we pulled in the past to deserve being locked up in here."

"Fair point."

In the distance, a group of five soldiers headed toward them. Their rifles gleamed in the morning sun.

Matthew strained his eyes. "Fuck . . . this doesn't look good."

The soldier on the left began shouting something in Vietnamese, to which the other men joined in. They were all highly animated. As they came closer, yelling and gesturing with their hands, the man in front raised his rifle and pointed it at Matthew.

"Wait. Wait! You can't d-do this," Matthew began, stuttering, backing into the corner of their keep. "Your government has signed a treaty. This is not—"

But his words were cut short by a single bullet that tore through his face and blew a hole out the back of his head.

A thick, wet blood cloud filled the cage.

Fletcher closed his eyes and waited for his bullet. The thoughts that ghosted into his mind were no different from the ones that kept him from his sleep.

His girls and Jack.

Sixty-four

The shot never came. In its place was a callous, almost caustic laughter.

By the time Fletcher wiped the blood from his face, the soldiers had already opened the cage and were removing Matthew's body. Their tactics were clear: The Australian's murder had been punishment for Fletcher's silence, a final reminder that death was closing in on him. One of the men made a comment, and the others laughed again. Fletcher felt like lunging at them and clawing out their throats, but had little strength to draw on. He was not at all concerned about being overpowered and killed, but rather of appearing weak in front of them. He decided that when they finally decided to shoot him, he would take the bullet with a smile.

It would prove a hollow victory, he knew, but it would surely stick in their throats.

The shooter tapped the barrel of his rifle and blew a kiss at Fletcher.

Then, one by one, the soldiers filed away, dragging Matthew's bloodied body behind them. Fletcher felt cold, despite the blistering morning sun on his back.

Although they had known each other only a short while, Fletcher had grown fond of Matthew. He was a kind and warm man and had managed to remain upbeat despite their circumstances. He had a young son back home in Perth of whom he spoke sometimes for hours on end. In letters to him before his capture, Matthew had planned a month-long camping trip with the boy. The prospect of which, Fletcher knew, had kept him going.

And now he was gone, his child forever lost to him.

Fletcher leaned forward and, using his hand like a spade, dug briefly into the sand in front of him. Moments later, he pulled out a compass Matthew had managed to stow away after his capture. He had planned to use it after they escaped—another ambition that would remain unfulfilled. Fletcher turned it over and stared at the name carved onto its casing: BRIAN. The etching was so deep, Fletcher imagined Matthew had spent days following the curvature of his son's name. He realized then, just as he had with Craig Fallow, that if he somehow managed to find his way home, he would have another letter to write. The chances of that, though, were almost nothing.

As the morning progressed, Matthew Summers quickly assumed his position in Fletcher's psyche as the latest inhabitant to pry at his sanity. It was becoming a crowded space.

Fletcher stared out through the bars and noticed Lee Tao heading toward him. He was carrying something in his arms, but it was hidden under a dark cloth. Despite his frame of mind, he was relieved the young man was still alive.

As Lee approached the cage, he bowed his head as a mark of respect at Matthew's death. "I sorry about your friend, Mr. Fletcher," he offered quietly. His eyes traced the bamboo frame, which was now coated dark brown from the dried blood. "He should not have died. This is wrong. You no hurt?"

"I'm all right."

"I bring soup and special food."

He removed the cloth and presented another bowl of rice, marginally smaller than the one before, and a large cup of soup.

"Lee . . . I'm very grateful for this, but they'll kill you if they find out what you're doing."

"I don't care. I hate this life. I rather . . . be dead." His optimism from the previous day had all but evaporated.

"Listen to me," Fletcher said, shifting closer to him. "The war is over. You could return to your village now. They wouldn't go after you. You can find your wife and start over."

"No more village left. My wife gone. I saw in your eyes."

"You saw nothing in my eyes! I really don't know about the village. It could still be there. Your wife might still be alive."

"Soldiers say it . . . burned."

"They're probably lying! Go see for yourself."

Lee ignored his comments, refusing to allow himself hope. "Must eat, Fletcher, please."

"Why? Why are you doing this? They're going to kill me anyway!"

Lee shook his head. "No. I help you."

"Help me what?"

Lee searched for the correct words. "To . . . go away."

Fletcher again marveled at how this relative stranger was willing to risk so much for him. "No escape, Lee. This is the end."

"No, you still have far to live."

"It's all right, Lee. I should've died a long time ago."

"No, you must live."

"Why? What makes you say that?"

"I was part of patrol when we find you sleeping. I watched. I saw."

Fletcher hadn't seen any of the men's faces at the time of his capture. Even if he had, he wouldn't have remembered. "I don't understand—"

"You must escape. He need you."

"Who needs me?"

"He hurt badly . . . but is still alive."

Fletcher felt his face go numb.

"Yellow dog. I saw him last night at river. He been following you."

Sixty-five

Fletcher couldn't believe what he had just heard. Could it be possible? Was Jack really still alive? "Are you sure, Lee? How do you know it was my dog?"

"Yellow," Lee replied, pinching the skin on his arm. "It's your dog."

"But he was shot!"

"No, soldier tried to shoot him, but missed. Your dog run away."

"Jesus Christ! He's okay?"

"His legs hurt, but he still able to walk little, little." Lee illustrated with his arms, then smiled warmly. "He walks for you, Mr. Fletcher."

Suddenly a voice called out from the distance, and Lee leapt to his feet. A brief but intense look washed over his face. "I wish I live in your country. In America, you are free."

Fletcher didn't know how to respond.

"No hope here, just death," Lee said, then spun away. "Please . . . must eat. Food save you."

And then he was gone, running toward the voice that had summoned him, every inch a prisoner himself.

Fletcher's hands were trembling. His skin tingled with energy.

Jack was alive.

It was a miracle he wasn't killed.

When he had calmed down sufficiently, he looked down at the food. What had been a lingering, almost distant hunger was now a ravenous appetite. Alternating with the soup, he grabbed handfuls of rice and forced it into his mouth. The food tasted heavenly. He was nearing the bottom of the bowl when he felt something cold and hard push against his fingers. He quickly fished out the foreign object.

He stared at it disbelievingly and then slowly heard himself laugh. Was he losing his mind? Was it all a dream?

The food will save you . . .

It was a long, thin strip of metal.

It was a blade.

Sixty-six

That night, Fletcher used the thin blade to painstakingly saw through a dozen of the thick bamboo bars to within a few centimeters of removing them completely. It was a far more difficult task than he had envisaged. He was tempted to try to escape right there and then, but knew it was too risky. It would soon be daylight. He would have to wait until the following evening to break out. He only hoped Jack could survive another day without him. It took every inch of his resolve to remain in the cage; his instincts told him that he should leave immediately and take his chances, but he knew that if he could wait it out until nightfall, they would have a far better chance of making a clean break.

He was massaging his hand to try to relieve some of the cramp, when he heard movement at the back of the cage.

It was Lee, his face etched with concern. "You must go now, Mr. Fletcher!" he urged, his chest heaving. He was struggling to catch his breath.

Fletcher scrambled toward him. "Lee . . . what're you doing here? What the hell's going on?"

"They going to shoot you! I heard . . . I heard."

"Jesus—"

"Did you use knife?"

Fletcher nodded. "They're going to know you gave it to me."

"No. I put handle in other soldier pocket. They think he guilty. He is bad man; I don't care about him."

"I still don't understand, Lee—"

"No more time for talk! Must go now!"

"But—"

"Hurry . . . hurry."

"All right, Lee, all right! But first answer one question for me."

"What?"

"Do you want to leave this place? Do you really want a life in America?"

Lee's eyes widened, and a glimmer of hope flickered across his face. "Must . . . hurry." Fletcher had his answer.

He reached through the cage and grabbed Lee's shoulder. "I'll come back for you, Lee. I'll take you to America. You have my word. Just stay alive, and I'll find you."

Lee bowed his head and pulled out a thick brown sack from under his shirt. "All food I could get for you. Now go . . . go!"

Fletcher crawled across to the far side of the cage, where he had sawed through the bamboo struts and kicked them out. He squeezed through the gap and replaced the bars behind him. If he was lucky, they wouldn't come for him for another hour or so.

As he turned around, Lee was standing in front of him. Instinctively, Fletcher embraced the young man.

"Your dog under trees over there," Lee said, pointing to an area across the river, away from the main bungalows. "He waiting for you."

Sixty-seven

Despite the approaching dawn, the sky was still a rich black. Running hard, Fletcher hunched over as he approached the trees. *"Jack . . . Jack . . . Jack,"* he whispered loudly.

There was no sign of him. Fletcher scrambled from tree to tree, trying to discern shapes between the different layers of shadow, but it was almost impossible. The foliage above him was blocking out what little light there was.

"Jack!"

Still nothing.

Had he died during the night? A feeling of dread gnawed at him. He called out again, louder this time.

Finally, a faint whimpering sound issued from somewhere behind him.

He spun around. "Jack! Where are you?" he pleaded, almost hysterical. About twenty yards to his left, the Labrador emerged from between two trees. His back legs were buckled uselessly under his body, and he was using his front legs to drag himself into a patch of moonlight.

Fletcher dropped down next to him and scooped him up in his arms. He buried his face into the fur around his neck, partly to drown out the sound of his own crying and partly because he needed to feel Jack, to make sure he was real. "I thought I'd lost you."

After holding him for a few moments, Fletcher pulled out of the embrace. Beyond Jack's pain, he could see the happiness in his eyes. It all seemed unreal, an impossible scene. "You tracked me, buddy. I'm so proud of you! Well done."

Jack lifted his head and licked the side of Fletcher's neck.

"What's wrong with your legs?" he then asked, as if expecting a reply.

Jack's back paw, still bandaged, had swollen up like a baseball, but his other hind leg looked all right. Why wasn't he able to walk at all? Fletcher wondered. As his eyes followed the curve of Jack's legs, he suddenly realized what the problem was. Since their separation, his right hip had somehow dislocated. Knowing precious little of how to restore a dislocated joint, but having no choice, Fletcher took hold of his dog's leg and gritted his teeth. He kissed Jack on the head and then twisted the leg and forced it into the joint.

Jack bucked at the sudden explosion of pain and then collapsed onto his side.

"Sorry, sorry, boy. It's over. I think it's back in. Just rest for a minute," he said, gently stroking his head.

As he allowed Jack some time to recover from the shock, he weighed their options. The night sky was now beginning to peel away from the horizon. They had the little bit of food Lee gave them and Matthew's compass, but still had at least fifty miles to travel just to reach Thailand. They had no map, no medicine, and would soon be hunted by their captors. That, and Jack couldn't walk.

Fletcher knew that if they were to stand any chance of surviving, they would have to run. He rose to his feet and lifted Jack in his arms. Taking a deep breath, he looked up at the sky. "You've taken everything from me. Just help me this once . . . *please.*"

Sixty-eight

By the time the sun had risen above the mountains, Fletcher estimated they had made at least six or even seven miles. At first, he had been surprised by his stamina, particularly since he hadn't eaten properly in weeks, but now he was beginning to tire. Jack had felt light initially, but now weighed heavily in his arms. It didn't help that the sack of food Lee had given him, which he had tied around his right shoulder, was pounding against his rib cage. The worst headache of his life wasn't making matters any easier either. On a positive note, his feet had healed well over the past few days, far better than he had expected. All that remained now was a distant ache as his boots fought for purchase on the slippery ground. His immediate concern now was water—or more accurately, the lack thereof. Although he was desperately thirsty, he was far more concerned about Jack. It was unlikely he'd had anything to drink since they were separated. To make matters worse, the sky overhead was clear. There were no immediate signs of rain, and they had not yet encountered a single water source.

By running, he knew he was taking a massive risk of crossing a wire or falling headlong into a trap, but prudence was simply not an option anymore. The clock was ticking. He had to put as much distance between himself and his captors as possible. To further compound matters, the infection in Jack's paw had clearly spread to the rest of his body and was slowly poisoning him.

He needed urgent medical help if he was to survive.

Despite this, however, Fletcher simply had to stop to rest for a while. His back was aching, and his throat was burning from the exertion. He still felt feverish. He lay Jack down and took a moment to catch his breath. The food sack had rubbed his skin raw under his arm, and he took the opportunity to swap it onto his left shoulder. As he untied the knot, it occurred to him that the sack was unnaturally heavy.

Maybe Lee had packed in some soup, he suddenly thought.

He quickly unfolded the cloth. Inside were two loaves of bread, a jar of rice, and a canister of water. The discovery took his breath away. He felt close to tears again. He knew that if by some miracle they made it to safety, he would owe much of it to Lee. Unscrewing the lid off the canister, he tilted Jack's head back and carefully funneled the precious water into his mouth. He could not afford to spill even a single drop. Jack battled to swallow at first, but then took in the water comfortably. Fletcher watched as his eyes came alive.

"That's it, Jack. Drink."

After Jack had accounted for a third of the canister, Fletcher took two long sips of his own and replaced the lid. He wished they could have more, but knew they could afford to drink only enough to stay alive.

Survival was now a race.

Sixty-nine

The afternoon sailed by like a small boat adrift at sea.

All that Fletcher remembered was putting one foot ahead of the other and trying his utmost to remain upright—a feat he managed most of the time. His arms had become ungainly leaden weights, and his back ached as if his spine had been supplanted with a column of burning lava. He kept peering over his shoulder, expecting to see soldiers charging up behind him, but each time there was nothing in his wake.

Did it mean they weren't coming after him? The war was over. Why should they care about one escaped prisoner? Given the terrain, they would have to pursue him on foot. How far would they go before they lost interest? Not too far, he hoped.

As the sun dipped over the trees ahead of him, he began to search for a place to spend the night. Initially he had planned to keep going, but now knew it wasn't possible. He needed to give his body at least a few hours to rest. Besides, in his current state, he would have no chance against a trip wire or trap at night. It wasn't worth the risk.

He noticed a slight vale under some heavy foliage some fifty yards to his left. If his head hadn't felt so heavy and cumbersome, he probably would've missed it.

It looked perfect. The only way someone would find them was if they literally fell into the chasm themselves. He carefully stepped down, parting the roots and branches ahead of him. The hollow was just wide enough for both of them. He lowered Jack down gently onto his side and stretched out his arms. His biceps felt thick and swollen.

Looking down at Jack, he could see he was hurting from all the jarring—clearly in a world of pain. Fresh blood seeped through the bandage on his paw. Fletcher sat down, removed the sack from his shoulder, and fished out one of the loaves of bread. He broke off a piece for Jack and fed it to him. The dough was still soft. Jack took a while to swallow it, but eventually got it down. He had three more small pieces, but then refused to eat any more. Fletcher tried to give him some more water, but he turned his head away. Fletcher took a few small sips himself and then quickly ate more than half the loaf. His stomach swelled up like a football. He was relying on the carbohydrates to give him the energy he needed for tomorrow—for one final push.

He tried to get Jack to eat a little more, but he was not interested. It was a worrying sign.

As the jungle's nightlife began to stir, repeating the same evening customs and rhythms, Jack fell into a deep sleep. As if joined by an invisible tether, Fletcher followed after him.

Seventy

An intense cramp in his shoulder plucked Fletcher from his sleep. At first, he thought something was trying to grab him, and he instinctively swung out, connecting only with the rough bark of an adjacent tree. As he regained control of his senses, he realized what was happening. He reached for the inflamed joint and could feel the muscle spasm under his skin. Using his knuckles, he tried to massage away the cramp, but it refused to relent. It took the better part of ten painful minutes to ease.

It suddenly occurred to him that Jack had slept through the entire incident. Normally when they were out on an assignment, the slightest sound would wake him. Even a shift in the wind would rouse him from his sleep. Something was wrong. He pressed his hand against Jack's chest and felt for a heartbeat.

"Jack. Wake up, boy."

Nothing.

"C'mon, wake up."

He lifted his hand to Jack's nose. It was cold and dry.

"Jack . . . hey."

He grabbed the skin around the Labrador's neck and pulled.

As if trying to awaken from a powerful anesthetic, Jack swallowed heavily, but his eyes remained closed.

"Jack! Stay with me. Do you hear me?"

His ears pricked up, but still he hovered somewhere between sleep and oblivion.

Fletcher quickly sat him up and again tried to feed him. After a few minutes, he managed to get down another two pieces of bread and a sip of water. When he was done, he rested the Labrador's head on his thigh. He put one hand on his chest and the other two inches in front of Jack's nose.

The situation was desperate. Jack's condition was deteriorating by the minute. For the rest of the night, if by sheer will alone, he was going to make sure Jack kept breathing. "Don't give up on me now, Jack. Our journey's almost over. Please."

He looked up at the only square of night sky that was visible to him.

"Not tonight . . . that's all I ask of you. Just give me one more day."

Seventy-one

The morning took forever to arrive. When it finally did, Fletcher wasted no time. He carefully lifted Jack up and climbed out of the vale. Jack had slept peacefully enough, but his condition was dire. In the final hours before sunrise, he had picked up a worrying tremor and his breathing had become labored. He remained in a half sleep.

Although Fletcher no longer had the luxury of a map, he didn't need one. They simply had to travel west. All that mattered now was moving as quickly and efficiently as possible. He estimated they had at least twenty miles to travel just to reach the Thailand border. From there, however, there was no way of telling how much farther they would have to hike to find help. If, indeed, there was any to be found.

This could still be their undoing, he knew.

Despite protests from his arms and shoulders, he began a slow jog. By midday he needed to, at the very least, have crossed over the border. Jack wouldn't make another night without medical help, of that he was certain. As Fletcher trundled forward, he realized that his mind no longer seemed capable of complex thought. It appeared to process only basic needs and functions. He was able to control his motor coordination competently enough, but whenever he tried to think of a way out of Thailand or how he was going to smuggle Jack back home, his mind resisted him. Coordinates, time, distance traveled, food reserves, potential water sources, traps, and changes in Jack's condition were the only real items considered high priority. His mind was conserving energy, focused on keeping them alive. It was only about survival. Everything else was peripheral; his body was saving resources in every way it knew how. What wasn't required could simply not be drawn upon.

There was, however, one notable exception.

Like a continuous movie reel, images of Abigail and Kelly never totally escaped him. Sometimes they would be in the background, like the sound of the ocean lapping against a distant shore, while other times they drifted right up to him like an encroaching tide. Occasionally the images were so vivid, it seemed as though he could reach out and touch them. Favorite memories would be broadcast over and over again. The day he met Abigail, the red dress she was wearing. The perfumed scent of her skin when they first kissed. Their wedding day. Kelly's birth. Her first steps. Her first words. Her first day at school. As the memories drifted inexorably toward the crash, Fletcher tried to suppress them. But in the end, he was always left with the shell of a burning plane and the tortured screams of its victims.

By midday, Fletcher had taken to carrying Jack over his shoulder. His arms could no longer sustain the weight. Unfortunately, it meant a more painful ride for Jack. Each jarring stride was transferred through Fletcher's shoulder and into the Labrador's body. Thin rivulets of blood and other fluids from Jack's wound ran down Fletcher's chest. He had stopped earlier to rest and had taken the opportunity to try to clean Jack's paw, but it was pointless. Nothing he could do superficially was going to be of any real help. However, while inspecting his right hip, he had detected a large swollen pocket near his groin. As he applied pressure to it, a thick dollop of black blood oozed out from a small hole in the skin.

He had no idea what it meant, only that it wasn't good.

Not wanting to dwell on it, he continued on, but now, after only a short while further, they had to rest up again. Fletcher had been dreading the stop, as they were about to finish the last of their water. Jack would be given two sips, and he would take one. On the positive side, he was confident they had covered at least twenty miles. He believed they would cross over into Thailand at any moment.

Perhaps they already had.

He kept searching for signs that they were no longer in Laos, but the terrain never changed. Several times he stopped, believing he could hear activity from a nearby village, but each time he was mistaken. Once, he thought he had heard a child's voice, but it was only a bird.

His ailing mind was starting to play tricks on him again.

Seventy-two

How could they be lost?

They had been heading west all day, and still there was no sign that they were in Thailand—nothing to confirm they had left Laos. Fletcher felt as though the jungle had become a giant conveyor belt, and they had been drifting around in circles. Irrational as it was, he half expected to soon round a corner only to discover the Strip, deserted, ahead of them.

Was he finally losing his mind? Were they even heading west?

Was he still locked up in his bamboo keep?

He grimaced and felt the corner of his mouth split open. He tried to run his tongue over the cut, but there was no moisture left in his mouth; it felt like he hadn't swallowed in days. The minor discomfort, however, paled into insignificance when compared to his other complaints. He had large welts and blisters on his shoulders and arms from carrying Jack. His left knee had locked up, and the subsequent compensation in his stride had caused his right ankle to become swollen and sore. Still, the most pain stemmed from the infection in his throat—he was now starting to taste blood.

But this was all background noise.

Jack was dying.

What little life he had left was ebbing away. In Fletcher's mind, Jack's remaining hours had become dry sand; the more he tried to hold on to it, the quicker it slipped through his fingers. Soon it would all be gone.

Fletcher was becoming frantic. They were desperate for water. He had tried digging for it, but the muddy reward it offered was outweighed by both the time it wasted and the energy he expended to unearth it. He had even tried to tap certain roots, but his knowledge of the changing flora made it something of a lottery. A sip from a poisonous plant or the ingestion of the wrong berries could be fatal. He had been trained to trap rainwater from even the slightest drizzle, but that first required the heavens to participate. More surprising than the complete lack of rainfall, though, was the notable absence of available fresh water in the area. They had passed a swamp earlier, but Fletcher decided not to drink the noxious water for fear of contracting some form of gastrointestinal complaint. Given their situation, diarrhea could kill them in a matter of hours.

He was trying to deny his growing sense of disorientation, but there were now long stretches in his memory that he could not account for. He had blacked out twice, and his sense of paranoia was growing. He was convinced that a helicopter was doing sweeps over the area. It would swoop down low and hover just above him. It had to be looking for them.

Somehow, it could see through the trees.

Each time he heard the swish of its blades, he would scramble for cover and wait for it to leave, but the chopper seemed determined to hunt him down—as if preternaturally aware of their presence.

Was it real? As the thought infected his mind, he suddenly stopped walking. Through the trees, a bright orange glow reflected on the leaves. He rubbed his eyes then slowly moved toward the light. Carefully, he parted the branches ahead of him.

What he saw was madness.

His own.

His wife and daughter were walking together through the jungle ahead of him. Their bodies were engulfed in flames.

Seventy-three

Abby . . . Kelly!" Fletcher cried out, his voice raw and hoarse. He had to get them on the ground to douse their flames. Their clothes, their skin, their hair—everything was ablaze. He could smell their burning flesh. But the harder he chased after them, the farther away they moved. "Abigail . . . Kelly . . . stop . . . it's me! Please, we have to put out the flames!"

But they kept walking, gliding away from him. They turned suddenly to the right and headed down a steep slope. The area was thick with trees and bushes, but somehow it didn't impede them at all. Fletcher, still barely clutching on to Jack, plunged down the embankment after them. Branches clawed at his arms, at the skin on his face and chest. He was running as fast as he could, but still couldn't close the gap between them. They reached the bottom of the slope then quickly ascended up another short hill, moving with impossible speed.

"Why are you running away from me? Please . . . stop!" he pleaded.

As his words carried up toward them, they finally drew to a halt. Abigail was holding Kelly's hand, but still their backs were turned to him. Fletcher scrambled up behind them. "Yes! Yes . . . Abby . . . Kelly!"

He got within ten feet of them, close enough to feel the heat from the scalding flames, when they both vanished.

"No!" he screamed, collapsing on the spot where they had stood.

The earth was cool under his hands.

As he rubbed the soil between his fingers, a wave of common sense and coherence came to him. If there had been any doubt over his deteriorating mental state, it had been purged by the fiery apparition of his dead family. He stared down at Jack, who was now awake from the chase. The Labrador blinked wearily then closed his eyes again.

"I'm sorry. We're lost and I'm falling apart. There's no . . ."

But his words trailed off as something ahead of him caught his attention. Over the rise, in the distance, was a cluster of huts. Next to them, stretching beyond the trees were three old buildings. On the roof of one of the buildings was a flagpole.

The colors of Thailand flapped gently in the warm breeze.

Seventy-four

Fletcher stared at the scene below him for the better part of a minute. Twice he turned away—praying that when he looked again the village would still be there.

It was.

This wasn't a cruel apparition drawn from his imagination. The Thai flag seemed to beckon him forward.

"Jesus Christ . . ." he murmured, his hands trembling. Summoning up the last of his reserves, he cradled Jack in his arms and broke into a run. Tears streamed down his face. His vision was narrowing. He began to scream. His throat, dry and bleeding, was burning with each word. His foot stubbed up against a large root, and he fell down heavily, grazing the skin off both his knees and elbows. He hardly felt it. He scrambled back up and continued running. He had to hurry. He screamed again, louder now. Shielding Jack's face with his free arm, he charged headfirst into the branches of a row of trees that separated them from possible salvation.

The Thai people heard his strained screams and stopped what they were doing.

It was a typical village day. There were people manning food stalls; some were carrying baskets, riding bicycles, mending shoes. Children were playing at the feet of their parents. As one, they waited and listened.

Suddenly Fletcher burst into view. He took a few unsure steps, reached the sand road that bisected the village, and slumped onto his knees. His chest was heaving. What strength remained in his arms drained away, and Jack rolled gently onto the ground. The villagers watched in silence as Fletcher took a deep breath and shouted the same few words that had caught their attention in the first place.

"Please help me . . . my dog is dying!" he cried out.

The villagers, stunned by what they were seeing, did not move. All except one.

A girl, too young to appreciate the gravity and potential danger of the moment, let go of her mother's hand and ran toward him. Her mother shouted to her, but she kept coming. Lying on his side now, Fletcher watched through half-closed eyes as she approached him. She couldn't have been more than four years old. She was beautiful. Angelic. Her long black hair framed the biggest brown eyes he had ever seen. Her smile warmed his heart. She knelt down beside him and placed her hand gently on the side of his face. She rested her other hand on the top of Jack's back. Fletcher tried to speak to her, but could feel himself slipping away. His peripheral vision was already lost. He felt like he was drifting off; like an empty vessel floating on the current of a retreating river. His body was shutting down.

The sound of a man's screams, angry and frantic, punctuated the air. Fletcher looked over the girl's shoulder and saw two Vietcong soldiers running through the crowd. In Fletcher's mind's eye, they seemed to be moving in slow motion. As they reached the road, only feet away from him, they raised their rifles and shouted for the child to move. The mother quickly scooped up her daughter and disappeared into the crowd.

The soldier closest to Fletcher pressed the butt of his AK-47 into his shoulder and widened his stance.

Fletcher tried to lift himself up, but couldn't. He felt paralyzed, empty. He had nothing left.

But Jack did. The Labrador lifted up on his front legs and dragged himself toward the soldiers.

"No," Fletcher cried. He stretched out his arm to try to stop him, but Jack was already beyond his reach.

The soldier curled his finger around the trigger and took aim.

Jack snarled and tried to lunge at the man—but fell short, collapsing onto his chest.

Tears burned Fletcher's eyes as the soldier pulled back on the trigger. "Jack!" Fletcher screamed. "*Jaaaack*!"

A helicopter, flying fast and low, roared over the treetops. It was traveling at such speed, it seemed certain to crash into the building adjacent to them. The two soldiers immediately swung their rifles up at the chopper as it churned up a tumultuous cloud of dust and grass. As the Huey hovered above them, its blades cutting up the late afternoon sun, a loud voice issued from the chopper's broadcast system.

Fletcher recognized the message. It was in Vietnamese. It was a phrase they had often used during their missions. It meant "Put down your weapons or die."

He felt himself first laugh, then he sobbed like a small child.

How could it be? How was it possible?

The voice belonged to a man from another world, another time. It was unmistakable.

It was Rogan.

PART III

The Last Dance

Seventy-five

By the time Fletcher finally regained consciousness, two days had passed. His body felt like it had endured much of that time being pummeled with tire irons. He found himself lying on a thin mattress on the floor of a small wooden hut. As he surveyed the room, he noticed that the old thatch roof, suspended somewhat precariously above him, was draped in a ghostly veil of spiderwebs.

"I leave them up there to keep out evil spirits," a woman's voice offered. "They don't bother me, and I certainly don't bother them."

Fletcher rubbed his eyes. "Excuse me?"

"The spiderwebs. They insulate the room against unwanted spirits. At least that's what the locals believe. Who am I to question their wisdom, right?"

"I'm sorry, but who are you?"

"A friend of a friend." She smiled. As she stepped into the room, away from the glare of the doorway, Fletcher was able to get a clear look at her. She was an attractive woman, probably in her early thirties, and appeared to have some Asian blood in her, although her accent was distinctly American. She was exceptionally thin, dangerously so, with long black hair and a soft and kind face.

"My dog," Fletcher said, clearing his throat. "Please . . . do you know what happened to him?"

She stared at him, and her smile faded. "I rather think your friends should speak to you about that."

Fletcher felt his stomach tighten. "I just want to know if he made it."

The woman knelt down beside him and gently placed her hand on his shoulder. "Everyone's very happy that you made it." With that, she stood up and walked away.

"Please, miss . . . I need to know—" Fletcher began, but stopped when he saw shadows gather on the wall alongside the doorway.

Will Peterson was the first to enter, followed by Mitchell and Rogan. They were carrying Jack on a stretcher.

Fletcher's breathing stalled.

"Just tell me one thing," Rogan said. "How in Christ's name did you do it?"

"Lieutenant . . ."

"Please, Fletcher, it's Rogan. The war's over."

"Mitch . . . Will . . ."

Will smiled and Mitchell winked. "We thought you might want to see this flea bag."

Fletcher was unable to speak.

"We don't know how he does it, but he seems determined to hang around."

As they lowered the stretcher, Fletcher could no longer hold back his tears. "Jack," he whispered, gritting his teeth. "It's over. We made it."

The Labrador opened his eyes and, as he saw Fletcher, barked softly.

Fletcher pulled himself to the edge of his mattress and threw his arms around his friend. "How?" he asked, looking up. "How did you know where to find us?"

"Later," Rogan suggested, his own face bearing signs of emotion. "There's a hundred things we want to ask you, but right now you still need to rest. We'll talk through everything tomorrow."

Seventy-six

Early the following morning and despite not fully trusting his legs, Fletcher staggered out onto the wooden deck that surrounded the hut. All three men were sitting on rickety cane chairs, waiting for him.

"Morning, sunshine," Rogan said. "Pull up a chair."

"Thanks, but I think I'll stand. Test my legs for a while."

"Some coffee?" Will offered, handing Fletcher a mug.

"Shit yes," he answered. "Thank you."

The mug felt awkward and heavy in his hand, but its contents tasted heavenly. After a few quick sips, he looked up and noticed they were in a small clearing in the middle of a jungle. Large trees draped in thick vines surrounded them in a natural amphitheater. The vegetation, although similar to that of Vietnam, was somehow different. It conveyed a more even, tranquil atmosphere.

"I didn't dream the last few months, did I? There was a war in Vietnam?" Fletcher asked quietly.

"I've heard of it," Mitchell confirmed.

"And we took part in it?"

"Against our better judgment."

"All right, that's a start," he replied, bringing the mug back up to his lips. "So Jack and I really did hike out?"

"Close to three hundred and eighty miles, we've worked out," Will said. "You guys made it to a small village called Moyan in the southeast of Thailand, almost thirty miles inside the border. Quite a stroll, I think it's fair to say."

"Where're we now?"

"Officially?" Rogan asked. "Nowhere. Lost. Missing in action, presumed dead."

A smirk skimmed across Will's face. "We're twenty-five miles north of Moyan. How much of your ordeal do you remember?"

"Flashes mostly, pieces of a puzzle that don't quite fit together. Much of what I recall is a blur, and the little that remains intact, I don't really trust."

"Well, then, let's at least tell you what we know," Rogan stated, pulling out a chair. "You really may as well get comfortable. This might take a while."

For the next hour, Fletcher listened intently as the story unfolded. Some of it sparked his own memories, but most of it was new to him. He learned that after the incident on the Strip, Rogan had been arrested and imprisoned, but after pressure from various quarters, and given his exemplary service record, he was soon released. Using his contacts, he found out about an American soldier being captured in Laos and his subsequent escape. Suspecting it was Fletcher, Rogan managed to get hold of an out-of-service Huey that he had repaired and set up for flight. When Mitchell and Will caught wind of what he was planning, they returned to join Rogan and insisted on being involved in the rescue attempt. And so it began.

Without authorization, they started brief flights between Thailand and Laos. Initially, they dipped into the country for only minutes at a time, but their desperation soon inspired more bold incursions. Their search area, however, remained confined to a forty-mile radius around Laos's western border. Rogan was convinced that Fletcher would head for Thailand. It was the only logical move. Despite being shot at numerous times, they continued undaunted. After ten days, their breakthrough finally arrived.

"It was little more than blind luck in the end. We were on our way back from a sweep when Mitchell saw you, carrying Jack, running toward the village. By the time we turned the chopper around, two soldiers already had their rifles trained on you, but we managed to distract them before they could do any damage," Will explained.

"I remember hearing Rogan's voice through the helicopter's speakers, but that was it. What happened afterwards?"

"We picked you up and brought you back here. The lady you met yesterday is Shayna Sykes. She's part of the Red Cross movement here in Thailand. She also happens to be a doctor. She operated on Jack, using a combination of Western medicine, voodoo, and God knows what else to fight the infection in his leg. She had us fetching roots and sand and all sorts of shit. But it seems to have worked. The infection is beginning to clear—" Will paused, reluctant to break the bad news. "—but, Fletch, she doesn't believe he'll ever be able to walk properly again. We'll just have to wait and see how he recovers."

"I guess I can live with that." Fletcher nodded, just grateful that Jack was still alive. "How'd you find out about Shayna? Why'd she agree to help?"

"You wouldn't believe us if we told you," Mitchell said. "Let's just say our commander had a hand in things. He apparently spent some time in Thailand several years ago."

"Wilson helped us? He knows about all this?"

"Officially, no. The government would shit themselves if they found out what we've been doing. We're an international incident just waiting to happen."

"Wilson had something of an attack of conscience when he heard about what you did," Rogan explained. "So he made a few calls to some people he knows, and Shayna is the result of that."

"Unbelievable," Fletcher remarked, lifting to his feet and shuffling to the edge of the deck. He rested his hands on the damp wooden railing. "I have a memory of a helicopter doing sweeps over the Laos jungle. It seemed to always be there, floating, lurking in the back of my mind. I spent hours hiding from it. Maybe even days."

"You realize that was us?" Will said.

Fletcher nodded. "If only I had known it then."

"Don't beat yourself up. Everything worked out in the end."

Fletcher turned around and folded his arms. "Why'd you guys do it?"

"Well, I personally couldn't get enough of Vietnam," Rogan explained.

"Weather's great this time of year," Mitchell added.

Rogan stood up and walked over to Fletcher. "What you did for Jack might be the most remarkable thing I've ever witnessed. How could we turn our backs on that?"

"I'll never be able to properly thank you."

Rogan shook his head. "You don't have to. At some stage, we've all played a part in keeping each other alive. The point is it's all over now. I've made arrangements to fly us back home—Jack included. Three days from now, this will all be a memory."

Fletcher turned away and gazed out into the jungle. "I'm sorry."

"For what?" Rogan asked.

"For what I'm about to say."

"What's that?"

Fletcher hesitated. "I can't leave yet. There's something I still have to do."

Seventy-seven

"What the hell are you talking about?" Rogan demanded, grabbing the back of Fletcher's arm.

"Look, I'm sorry, but I made a promise to someone."

"What promise? What could possibly keep you here?"

"When I was captured in Laos, a man helped me escape. I would've died were it not for him."

"So? What's that got to do with you staying here?"

"I'm going back for him."

The group was quiet for a moment, as each of the men digested Fletcher's statement. "I gave him my word that I would return for him and bring him to America."

"Are you out of your fucking mind? You can't be serious?" Rogan said. "After everything we've been through?"

"I'm sorry, but I have to do this."

"We didn't risk our goddamn lives so you could just throw

yours away based on some ridiculous pact you made with one of your captors!"

"Who is this man?" Mitchell intervened.

"His name is Lee Tao. He was forcibly recruited from that small village we helped defend about five months ago. That's actually why he helped me in the first place: He recognized my face."

"Fletcher, when you're a POW, you'll sell your soul for a cup of warm piss. No one expects you to honor your word under those circumstances."

"He gave me a blade, which I used to escape. At great risk to himself. Without it, I would've died. How can I turn my back on that?"

"This is a joke, isn't it?"

Fletcher shook his head.

Rogan punched a hole in the back of his chair. "Christ! This is insane."

"I don't expect you to be happy about it, but I really don't have a choice. I couldn't live with myself if I didn't at least try to help him." Fletcher looked down at his hands and shrugged. "I gave him my word. That's all I have for you."

Rogan paced across the deck, his fists clenched at his sides. "How far into Laos is this camp?"

"Fifty-five, maybe sixty miles."

"How the hell are you planning on getting there?"

"Haven't thought that far yet."

"What's the protection like?"

"Pretty lightweight. No perimeter fencing, just three guard towers from what I could see."

"Soldiers?" Mitchell inquired.

"Maybe forty, but there could be more. Why?"

"Well, you better be sure. We'll need to know before we go."

"Before *we* go?"

"Gentlemen," Rogan sighed, looking to Mitchell and Will, "how do you feel about one last dance in our little slice of hell?"

Will thought for a moment. "I'll fly you wherever you need to go."

"One final twirl on the dance floor? Thought you'd never ask," Mitchell responded, bowing.

"No, forget it. I won't endanger—"

"The decision's made, Fletcher. We're playing this thing out together one way or the other. Besides, when the story of this crazy bullshit is told one day, I sure as hell don't want to be remembered as the asshole who walked away. I want to be there in the end, riding a fucking white horse."

"I don't know what to say."

"There's nothing to say. But before we take this any further, is there anything else we should know? Is there maybe a children's village in Saigon that you'd like us to rescue?"

Fletcher looked up at the sky. "Actually, there is something. Lee still has a wife in Vietnam. In that same village we helped protect. Don't know if she's still alive, but if she is, we need to get her out as well. What do you think of that, Rogan?"

"Fucking wonderful," he yelled, "and it's lieutenant again, Carson. Christ to hell!"

Seventy-eight

The remainder of the week was spent planning the rescue.

Mitchell managed to get his hands on an aerial shot of the camp, which, as Fletcher had suggested, showed only three watchtowers defending it and seemingly nothing else. Apart from a river, which guarded its western perimeter, its remaining boundaries appeared exposed.

Rogan picked at the rough skin on his lip. "It's too easy. There's something wrong here. What kind of camp doesn't raise a proper perimeter?"

"I passed another camp when Jack and I first reached Laos. It was pretty much the same story."

"There must be mines . . . has to be. How'd you get out?"

"I crossed the river. Jack was waiting for me under the trees on the other side."

"Then that's how we'll go in. No one leaves their front door open like that . . . even if the war's over."

Shayna Sykes stepped out onto the deck and tossed a dishcloth over her shoulder. "Would you boys like something to eat?"

"We'll infiltrate at around two in the morning; that should give us enough time to make it back."

"That'll be fine—most of the soldiers seemed to turn in hours before that."

"Don't mind me. I'm just the cook," Shayna sighed, retreating back into the hut.

Fletcher stroked the side of Jack's head. The canine was now sleeping peacefully on the stretcher alongside them. He was concerned that the Labrador hadn't yet stood up, or even tried to. The prospect of Jack never being able to walk again filled Fletcher with dread. It was a reality he might soon have to face up to, but just not right now. There was still an outside chance of him regaining some form of mobility. Besides, Jack had faced and overcome worse. Time would tell with him; it always did.

"How close can you drop us?"

"Probably about three or four miles out," Will calculated.

"Let's keep it at five to be safe," Rogan said, still studying the photograph. "Fortunately, from our initial searches we know most of the terrain fairly well. I'm confident we can fly in undetected."

"My job's the easy part. The rest is up to you guys. Are you not concerned about having to deal with traps at night?"

Fletcher gently massaged his bare feet, which were still bruised and tender. "I didn't encounter any after my escape—at least none that I saw. That doesn't mean there aren't any, but I think it's a damn sight safer than Vietnam."

"We'll have to take our chances."

Fletcher agreed. "When do you think Mitchell will be back?"

"I don't know, but if the woman's alive, Lord will find her. I have no doubt."

They had woken up two days earlier to discover that Mitchell had disappeared. He left a cursory note behind offering only four words as an explanation: *Gone for the wife.* He made no indication of what his plan was or when he expected to be back.

"I hope he's all right," Fletcher said.

"Lord's a lot like Jack, here. He can walk through a river of shit and come out clean the other side. He'll make it out."

Will clapped his hands and rubbed them together. "All right, then, everything's set. When do we dance?"

"Tomorrow night," Rogan answered, clearing his throat. "Let's finish this."

Seventy-nine

The water was surprisingly cold, considering the ambient temperature. Fletcher and Rogan waded halfway across the river and waited alongside a dense patch of reeds. The camp was quiet—almost unnaturally so. A lone soldier was sitting on top of the guard tower closest to them, but he appeared to be sleeping. His rifle, like his head, was casually propped up against one of the tower's support struts. In fifteen minutes, they hadn't seen any signs of a ground patrol; the area separating the various bungalows appeared deserted.

"You ready?" Rogan asked, scanning the camp with his binoculars.

"Let me go alone. There's no point in both of us going."

Rogan huffed and pushed forward. "Fuck off, Carson."

"Just once I wish you'd listen to me."

Together they crawled up the embankment and ran across to a large tree less than twenty yards away from the first bungalow. There were still no signs of activity anywhere. "What makes you think he's in this bungalow?"

"I saw him come in here at least twice a day."

"That doesn't mean it's where he sleeps, but I suppose we've got to start somewhere."

Pressing the butt of his rifle into his shoulder, Rogan turned and ran toward the front of the bungalow. Fletcher shadowed behind him. They stepped quietly up onto the raised wooden deck and listened for movement. Only the sound of water, dripping into pools at their feet, detracted from the silence.

"The door," Rogan whispered.

Fletcher stepped forward and quietly turned the handle.

The door opened with a slight creak, and the soft glow of the stars spilled inside.

Rogan moved purposefully through the doorway, swinging his M16 in a wide arc. As his eyes adapted to the darkness, he was able to make out two rows of about sixteen soldiers all sleeping soundly on the floor.

Fletcher immediately began to look for Lee. Some of the men were lying on their sides and stomachs, which made it difficult to see their faces. Using a torch that he had taped up with black cloth to diffuse the light, he quickly searched the first row and was halfway through the second when he found him.

Lee was still alive. The trip back had not been for nothing.

Rogan knelt down beside him. "On three."

Fletcher raised his thumb. "One . . . two . . . *three.*"

They both threw themselves on top of Lee. Fletcher cupped his hand tightly over the soldier's mouth while Rogan held down his legs.

Lee immediately tried to struggle free.

"Lee . . . Lee," Fletcher urged, trying to calm him down. "It's me. Look."

Lee's eyes, like the cusps of winter moons, locked on to Fletcher. The fight immediately drained out of him.

Fletcher removed his hand.

"Mr. Fletcher . . . how . . . what you doing here?"

"We've come for you."

"For me? I don't understand."

"To get you out of here," Fletcher explained, and then smiled. "I told you I'd come back for you."

Lee sat up and threw his arms around Fletcher as if they were old friends.

"All right, you two," Rogan interjected. "Let's go."

They quickly stood up and moved toward the door. They were about to step outside when Lee stopped.

"Wait." He turned around and went back to the area where he was sleeping. He quietly picked up a bag and placed it at the feet of the soldier next to him.

"What was that about?" Fletcher asked as he returned.

"He my friend. I want him to have my food and books."

Fletcher felt warm, despite his wet clothes. If he'd had any misgivings about returning for Lee before, they evaporated with that simple gesture.

Eighty

Back out on the deck, they surveyed the area for any signs of danger. There was still no indication of a patrol. As they prepared to make the short run to the river, Rogan noticed a change on top of the guard tower. The soldier, who'd been sleeping before, was now having a smoke. The tip of his cigarette glowed like a red star pinned against the night sky. "We're going to have to wait this out. Hopefully he'll finish his smoke and go back to sleep."

Sitting with their backs against the bungalow, under the shade of the eave, they watched as the crimson tip alternated between the guard's lap and his mouth. The more he smoked, the more animated he seemed to become. He would throw up his arms every minute or so, as if remonstrating with himself.

"What the hell is wrong with him?" Fletcher asked.

"He sick up here," Lee uttered, pointing to his head. "He very angry with everyone. He friend of war. Not happy to end war."

The man, now finished with the cigarette, flicked the burning stub over the side of the tower. Without warning, he turned on his search lamp and ran it across the bungalow. The light washed over them before they had a chance to react. The guard leaned forward, as if unsure of what the light had uncovered, then hastily reached over to raise the alarm.

"Jesus Christ! We have to go . . . now!" Rogan said, scrambling to his feet.

"Oh, fuck . . ." Fletcher spat out, grabbing Lee's arm.

As they ran, the guard opened fire on them, wildly emptying an entire clip in their direction. Sprinting as hard as they could, they threw themselves into the river and swam for the embankment. Fletcher glanced over his shoulder and watched as soldiers streamed out of their bungalows. In the confusion, they fanned out in all directions. A group of about fifteen men headed toward the river.

"They're coming! *Move!*" Rogan insisted, reaching the bank. Together they hurried behind a column of trees and continued into the bowels of the jungle.

"Where we going?"

"There's a helicopter waiting for us," Fletcher gasped, sucking in large mouthfuls of air. "Not far from here."

"We never make it. These soldiers very fast."

The familiar cackle of AK-47 fire ripped through the branches above them.

"Just fucking run!" Rogan called back.

Eighty-one

Rogan had called back, realizing the soldiers were gaining on them. "Those trees"—he gestured, pointing ahead—"get up them."

With the soldiers only a hundred or so yards behind, they each scrambled up a tree. As Fletcher hurried to get into a shooting position, his M16 slipped from his grasp and fell to the ground. It was a mistake, he knew, that could cost them their lives. There was no time left to climb down and retrieve it; the soldiers would come into view at any moment.

Lee, knowing they had no chance with only one rifle, decided to go after it. He jumped down from his position and hurried toward it. Just as he reached down, the first soldier rounded the corner. Fletcher watched in horror as the man lifted his AK-47 and pointed it at Lee. But before he could pull the trigger, Rogan shot him twice in the chest.

Lee grabbed the rifle and threw it up to Fletcher.

"Down, Lee!" Fletcher shouted as the other soldiers appeared.

The second man tripped over his dead compatriot, bunching up the group.

They never stood a chance.

From their elevated position, Rogan and Fletcher cut down the entire group within seconds. Their automatic fire all but obliterated them; the soldiers did not even manage a single meaningful volley in reply.

As the smoke filtered up through the trees, Lee stood up and walked over to the pile of bodies.

"Lee, wait, it's not safe . . . come back!" Rogan yelled.

Ignoring the warning, Lee circled halfway around the back of the group and drew to a halt. He sat down and raised his hands to his mouth.

"What's he doing?" Rogan asked, climbing down.

"I have no idea."

As they charged up behind him, it all became clear. Lying under a badly mutilated soldier was Lee's friend, the man he'd given his bag to.

"He was the only person who was . . . kind to me."

"I'm sorry, Lee. We had no way of knowing."

Lee ran his fingers over the man's lifeless face, closing his eyes. "It's not your fault. It's war. Terrible war."

Fletcher hunkered down next to Lee. "This is the end. It's all over now."

"In America there is no war?"

Rogan sighed. "Not like this."

Lee folded his friend's arms over his chest and stood up. "We leave this place?"

"Yes . . . we leave this place."

Eighty-two

The flight back to Thailand was an edgy affair. As long as they were over Laos, they were still at risk of being shot down. In spite of the darkness, Will flew at treetop height, swooping down into clearings as often as he could. Twice, the helicopter's skis clipped small branches, but neither Rogan nor Fletcher said a word; they trusted their pilot implicitly.

As the first signs of morning lifted the gloom, they crossed over into Thailand and put down in a small open area, barely wide enough to house the chopper. They jumped out and quickly hauled a large green and brown tarpaulin over the Huey. Above them, the day's first birds soared and wheeled across the navy sky, their song inviting the rising sun.

"Over here," Shayna called out. She was parked in an old jeep under a nearby tree.

"Where we going?" Lee asked.

"Somewhere safe," Fletcher said.

After a short drive, they pulled up in front of Shayna's hut. A tall, dark figure was standing casually in the doorway, waiting for them.

It was Mitchell.

"Mitch! You made it!" Fletcher clapped his hands together.

"Of course. I see you did, too."

Rogan swung his rifle over his shoulder and climbed out of the jeep. "What took you so fucking long, Lord?"

"Stopped to admire the shiny bullet shells on the side of the road, lieutenant."

As they approached the stairs, Mitchell looked toward Lee and nodded. "I've heard a great deal about you. Welcome."

"Thank you." He smiled. "I very happy to be here."

"Fletcher tells us you're to blame for saving his life."

Lee missed the joke. "Only after you all save my village. I very grateful for your help."

As they congregated together, Lee turned to Fletcher and bowed. "I want to thank you for coming to me, Mr. Fletcher. You sacrifice very much to help me, but . . ."

"What is it, Lee?"

"I sorry . . . I can't come away with you," Lee explained, lowering his head as an apology. "Not until I know for myself. Maybe you right. Maybe my wife got away . . . maybe she still alive. She mean everything to me. I cannot leave not knowing what happened to her. Please forgive me."

Mitchell leaned forward and placed his hand on Lee's shoulder. "We thought you might feel that way." He stepped away from the doorway, and an attractive, petite young woman appeared behind him. She kept her head down, seemingly afraid to look up.

Lee's eyes widened in surprise, and he threw his hands over his mouth. "Tay?" he managed.

"Lee," the woman replied, breathless, still reluctant to look up.

"Tay . . . Tay!" he repeated, and ran toward her. They embraced and collapsed to their knees, crying. Lee said something to her in Vietnamese, and she sobbed back her reply, repeating her answer over and over.

Fletcher, taken by the moment, glanced across at Shayna, who was fluent in several languages. "What did she say?"

Shayna dabbed the corners of her eyes with her shirtsleeve. "What we all dream our partners would say of us: 'I never stopped believing in you.' "

After Lee and Tay had finally ended their embrace, Mitchell explained how he had tracked down the coordinates of her village and then paid an old Vietnamese informant of theirs to go in and get her out. After a full day of walking and nearly two days of driving, the man finally delivered her to a small village on the outskirts of Saigon.

Mitchell looked up at Fletcher. "There's also some good news for you." He pursed his lips together and whistled loudly.

A moment later, Jack emerged in the open doorway, his tail wagging.

"Jack . . . you're walking!"

As if to prove it, he slowly weaved toward Fletcher.

Shayna shook her head in disbelief as the Labrador brushed past her. "This is impossible; I don't believe it. He shouldn't be able to stand, let alone walk. The bone density in his leg should not be able to support his weight."

"Jack has remarkable powers of recovery," Will said.

"No, you don't understand. Recovery is one thing—this animal shouldn't be mobile. I knew he would never walk again; I just didn't have the heart to tell any of you."

"He's really quite something."

"You're not hearing me: *Him walking is medically impossible!*"

"When it comes to Jack, anything's possible," Mitchell corrected her.

"He's barely limping."

"If you knew his past, you wouldn't be so surprised."

"His past?"

"Shot at least four times—twice by us—lost several pints of blood. He's a survivor," Mitchell explained.

"Where did he come from?"

Fletcher looked up at Shayna, and a knowing look eased onto his face. "You wouldn't believe me if I told you."

Mitchell bent over to pat Jack as he passed. "What do you mean, Fletch? Did you find out which unit he was attached to?"

"No, he was never part of any unit in Vietnam. The past few weeks have made me understand something. Although I've no way of proving it and you're probably going to think I've lost my mind, I know it's true. Jack didn't come from Vietnam."

"Then where?" Rogan pressed.

"He came from somewhere . . . *else.*"

Will frowned. "You've lost us."

Fletcher knelt down as Jack reached him. He closed his eyes and rested his forehead gently against the side of the Labrador's neck. "Travis was right. He always said Jack never belonged here, something about the look in his eyes. I believe I now understand why. My daughter, Kelly, died in a plane crash three days before she would have turned seven. She kept begging my wife and I for this one special birthday present. I've never known her to be so insistent; she was adamant about it. She wanted a Labrador. She even had a name picked out."

Will closed his eyes. "Jack?"

Fletcher nodded in return and then raised his head. "I've never been more certain of anything in my life: My daughter sent Jack to me."

Epilogue

Chicago
Ten years later

More than a decade had slipped by since Fletcher first had cause to pass through Hampton Lane's front gates, but still the cemetery appeared the same. Many of its tenants lining the roads had been at rest for longer than Fletcher had been alive. Only the trees, now tall and imperious, were evidence of the passing years.

As their cavalcade wound toward the southern end of the cemetery, Fletcher cast his mind back to the war and their last few days in Thailand. Most of his memories of that time had faded badly, like an old photograph worn yellow by the sun. He recalled how, shortly before they left for America, they had all agreed to keep in touch. As it turned out, he had spoken to Will and Mitchell only a handful of times over the years, and just twice to Rogan. Despite all they had been through—everything they had endured—he always knew their friendships could not be sustained on the outside. Their bonds had been forged in another world. In the pale, thin light after the war, their relationships quickly wilted.

Stepping out of his car, Fletcher headed up the grassy embankment toward the large maple tree that still regularly haunted his dreams. As always, he lowered down and gently placed a white rose across each of his girls' graves.

Every visit still hurt him deeply; the wounds had never quite healed. He knew they never would. They were now just a part of his life that he tried to deal with as best he could. As he waited for the rest of the group to join him, he tried not to look into the hollow darkness of the newly dug grave alongside him. He knew that if he did, it would drain away what little courage he had summoned for the burial.

"You all right?" Marvin asked, joining him at his side.

"No, but thanks for coming. I really appreciate it."

"Nothing could've kept me away."

Fletcher tried to thank him again, but the words died in his throat. The emotion of the day was already weighing on him. Marvin had been a loyal friend to him over the years, both before the crash and in the wreckage after it. He felt guilty about the one-sided nature of their relationship and had often wondered why Marvin had stood by him so resolutely. Several weeks following his return to America, Marvin persuaded him to return to journalism. He even managed to get him to freelance for the newspaper again and then, after a while, encouraged him to compose letters to his girls. Fletcher was skeptical of the idea at first, but eventually agreed to try it. It was almost impossible in the beginning, but after a few weeks, the words came a little easier. Eventually he was able to write freely. Ultimately, it proved to be an extremely cathartic experience. He told them about the horror of Vietnam—but also how hope can exist in the darkest of places—and of how much he missed them, how deeply he felt their absence. He even wrote about his attempted suicide and confessed that, as much as he tried to deny it, for a long time after the crash, thoughts of taking his own life never strayed far from his mind. But that had slowly changed. A year after returning from the war, Shayna Sykes arrived unannounced on his doorstep. In the months that followed, they became close friends and, eventually, lovers. He had found a safe space in his heart where he could love Shayna without tarnishing Abigail's memory. He finally accepted that it was okay to give himself to another woman. Just as she had brought him back from the brink of death in Thailand, Shayna gradually taught him how to live again. She loved him dearly. Sometimes, he felt, more than he deserved. She would even accompany him to the graves of his girls sometimes, but decided not to join him on this occasion. This was their day.

Lee and Tay were next to reach the gravesite.

For them, their first taste of America had been difficult. There weren't many people prepared to welcome Asians into their neighborhoods after the war. But like everything, things improved with time. Prejudices softened; hatred dissipated. When the time was right, Fletcher helped them open a small art gallery in the heart of Miami, which after a few difficult years, was now turning a tidy profit. They were both talented artists, and their work was becoming highly sought after. The free life Lee had always dreamt of was now a reality. If that wasn't enough, they were blessed with two wonderful children: a boy and a girl. As their neighbor, Fletcher was able to watch them grow—little in his life meant more to him.

Fletcher looked back and watched as Mitchell, Will, and Rogan came up the hill. It occurred to him, with some irony, that Mitchell was still walking in front . . . ever the point man. He still had his thick mane of long black hair and the same look of madness lurking deep within his eyes. After the war, he joined up with an underground government agency. He was not permitted to talk about the details of his job, and Fletcher had no desire to ask. He knew only too well who Mitchell Lord was.

Will Peterson followed with a slight limp—a permanent keepsake from his time as a hostage in Vietnam. During the day, he ran a successful charter airline with over a dozen aircraft under his control. At night, he drank. More than he ought to, Fletcher had heard, a lot more. He married twice, but both unions had failed. Vietnam, it appeared, continued to cast its dark shadow over him.

Walking slowly at the back was Rogan. Fletcher had never quite come to terms with what his lieutenant had done for him. From the day on the chopper and the rescue in Thailand to traveling back into the war to save a stranger. They had come a long way together. In the outside world, Rogan lived alone in a small flat in Detroit, working as a night-shift security guard at a chemical factory. Fletcher wondered what kind of dark thoughts plagued his friend's mind in the small hours of the morning. The hostile reception Rogan received upon returning from Vietnam was too much for him to bear. Most of the soldiers suffered some form of abuse, but for Rogan it was different. He was a patriot who believed wholeheartedly in what they were fighting for. He considered their cause honorable and just. The American public's lack of appreciation of his and his fellow soldiers' efforts affected him more than most. It was a betrayal. It stripped away his spirit. That such a courageous man—a powerful leader—should today hold such a menial position seemed a great tragedy to Fletcher. Rogan still gave the appearance of a man who was strong and fit, but there was now a heaviness about him that was troubling. He carried the look of a damaged man.

Yet another casualty of Vietnam.

Fletcher stepped forward and took a deep breath. As he looked at the people around him—with whom he'd been through so much—he struggled to contain his emotions.

"Before we left Thailand all those years ago, we made a pact that regardless of where we were, we would all come together one last time. It means a great deal to me that you've each kept your word and made it here today, as I knew you would.

"After we left, I came out to Miami, initially to honor a promise I made to Travis, but as it turned out, I could never find a reason to leave. The city has become not only my home, but home to Lee and Tay and their two children as well. Most days, when the weather is good, Lee and I play chess out on his porch. I haven't won many games, but in the course of being regularly beaten, I've been privileged enough to watch his children grow. His daughter, Mia, started school this year. I can't tell you the pleasure that brings me. His son, Kim, begins school next fall. He loves baseball and giving high fives when the mood takes him, which is often. Both Lee and Tay are successful artists now with their own thriving gallery: The Fat Lady. Each of you played a role in making their lives here possible. Lee asked me to specially convey his and Tay's ongoing thanks and appreciation for everything you've done for them."

Both Lee and Tay bowed, and each of the men nodded in recognition.

"Okay. I'm going to do my best to make it through this. Please bear with me," Fletcher announced, taking a moment to compose himself. "When we made this pact, I always prayed that today would be a great many years away. As it turned out, I was given ten full years. You always want more, but it's probably longer than I deserve. I want you to know that Jack was never sick a single day in all that time. Each morning, regardless of what commitments the world demanded from us, we would always go down to the beach. Jack loved to swim in the breakwater and run after seagulls. His exuberance never waned. I don't think he ever really wanted to catch the seabirds; he just enjoyed the chase. In his last few months, when his hips began to fail, I would carry him to the beach and we'd stare out over the ocean together. Sometimes I'd be late for appointments, but it never mattered. There's nothing like surviving a plane crash and living through a war to give you some perspective on what's important." He paused, his voice faltering. "It was a beautiful, warm morning when he died. Just as I had carried him in Southeast Asia . . . so he slipped away in my arms. I must've sat on that beach holding him for hours. I remember stroking the side of his face until my fingers became numb. It was Lee who eventually found us. He knew exactly where to look. Although I don't remember it happening, he gently pried Jack from my arms, and Tay helped me to her car. I can't tell you where we drove that day, just that I cried all the way. I take great comfort in the last years of Jack's life. I know that he loved each and every day we shared—God knows I did. But . . ." he said, no longer able to restrain his grief, "it doesn't make his passing any easier. I . . . I guess I just miss my friend."

The group crowded around Fletcher, and Rogan placed his hand on his shoulder. Fletcher rested his own hand on top of his lieutenant's, but kept his head bowed. For a while, they were quiet as Jack's coffin was moved into position.

Ordinarily, no cemetery would allow an animal to be buried on its premises, but the caretaker of Hampton Lane had become a close friend of Fletcher's over the years. He had lost both his boys to Vietnam. When he heard the news of Jack's passing, he immediately offered Fletcher a plot next to his girls.

Mitchell walked across to a basket that was filled with a dozen white roses. He chose one, kissed it, and gently placed it on top of Jack's coffin. Marvin, Lee, and Rogan each followed suit. Fletcher could hardly see anymore. His tears had blurred and distorted his vision. He wanted to say more—there was so much more that needed to be said—but he knew the words would fail him. He stumbled up to the grave and placed Jack's leash on top of his coffin. "I wish we could spend just one more day together," he managed, then whispered, "Just to watch you run, Jack . . ."

Overcome by the moment, Tay ran up behind Fletcher and wrapped her arms around him. Together they watched as Jack was lowered down. When the coffin had come to a stop, each of the men shoveled a measure of sand into the grave until there was little of his coffin left to see.

Fletcher felt exhausted, drained; his head was reeling.

He felt on the verge of passing out.

As Lee and Tay led him away, he looked back and saw that both Rogan and Mitchell were kneeling next to Jack's cross. They were reading his epitaph.

Fletcher closed his eyes and read along with them.

JACK

I now know that Vietnam could never claim you.
Some souls burn too bright to be lost to the darkness.
Yet, as we part, know that our journey is not at an end.
Just as you found me, I will seek you out again.
Run to her, Jack, she's waiting for you.
I'll be along in a while.
Ruush.

Fletcher

Author's Note

F*inding Jack* is a tribute to the Vietnam war dogs, many of whom gave their lives to protect American and allied soldiers. Shortly after troops began to pull out of the war, it's believed the U.S. government ordered that the dogs be left behind. It was proving too expensive to transport them home. They were labeled as "surplus military equipment" and left to fates unknown.

Some were handed over to the South Vietnamese, but many were left to die. In the end, it's estimated that some four thousand dogs were sent to serve in Vietnam. It's believed they saved the lives of more than ten thousand soldiers.

Fewer than two hundred dogs made it home.

May we never forget their sacrifice. And if you can remember Jack, then you can remember all the dogs.

I hope you do.

2/21/11